LOVE STORY
The Unauthorized Biography of Jennifer Love Hewitt

Most Berkley Boulevard Books are available at special quantity discounts for bulk purchases for sales promotions, premiums, fund-raising or educational use. Special books, or book excerpts, can also be created to fit specific needs.

For details, write: Special Markets, The Berkley Publishing Group, 375 Hudson Street, New York, NY 10014.

LOVE STORY
The Unauthorized Biography of Jennifer Love Hewitt

MARC SHAPIRO

BERKLEY BOULEVARD BOOKS, NEW YORK

If you purchased this book without a cover, you should be aware that this book is stolen property. It was reported as "unsold and destroyed" to the publisher, and neither the author nor the publisher has received any payment for this "stripped book."

LOVE STORY

A Berkley Boulevard Book / published by arrangement with
the author

PRINTING HISTORY
Berkley Boulevard edition / December 1998

All rights reserved.
Copyright © 1998 by Marc Shapiro.
Cover design by Steven Ferlauto.
Cover photograph by Alan Levenson/Corbis.
This book may not be reproduced in whole or in part,
by mimeograph or any other means, without permission.
For information address: The Berkley Publishing Group,
a member of Penguin Putnam Inc.,
375 Hudson Street, New York, New York 10014.

The Penguin Putnam Inc. World Wide Web site address is
http://www.penguinputnam.com

ISBN: 0-425-16755-0

BERKLEY BOULEVARD
Berkley Boulevard Books are published by The Berkley Publishing Group,
a member of Penguin Putnam Inc.,
375 Hudson Street, New York, New York 10014.
BERKLEY BOULEVARD and its logo
are trademarks belonging to Berkley Publishing Corporation.

PRINTED IN THE UNITED STATES OF AMERICA

10 9 8 7 6 5 4 3 2 1

This book is dedicated to the two LOVES in my life: my wife, Nancy, and my daughter, Rachael. My mother, Selma. My dad and mother-in-law in heaven. My hardworking agent, Lori Perkins, Barry at Berkley, and all the forces that combine to keep us young at heart.

CONTENTS

ACKNOWLEDGMENTS	ix
INTRODUCTION: *Love Song*	1
ONE: *Love Walks In*	9
TWO: *Lucky in Love*	23
THREE: *Love on the Small Screen*	41
FOUR: *Love Joins the Party*	59
FIVE: *Love's in Love*	77
SIX: *Love on the Run*	95
SEVEN: *Love Unlimited*	113
EIGHT: *Love Notes*	127
NINE: *Love on the Line*	129

ACKNOWLEDGMENTS

The following people willingly gave of their time and memories: Jim Wynorski, Ginger Wells, Pat Pate, and Freddie Harrell. Special thanks to them. Also a big-league thank you to Anthony "Junket Junkie" Ferrante for the loan of his *I Know What You Did Last Summer* tapes.

The following magazines and newspapers contributed to the cause: *Seventeen, TV Guide, Teen, Premiere, Variety, US, People, Entertainment Today, Entertainment Weekly, Soap Opera Update, Los Angeles Times, Dramalogue, Movieline,* and *The Hollywood Reporter.* Also big kudos to the book *Party of Five: The Unofficial Companion* by Brenda Scott Royce.

INTRODUCTION
Love Song

Jennifer Love Hewitt kissed Will Friedle good night.

It was a friendly kiss, a first-date kiss. But later that night, alone in her room, Jennifer was already hoping to see him again. They seemed to have so much in common. They were two of the hottest young actors on television. Will had the kind of fun-loving attitude she adored. It had been a perfect evening.

"I thought Will was the coolest guy," Jennifer said later, reflecting on those postdate feelings. "It just seemed to me that we both had so much in common."

She knew she had to see him again. But she also knew that she didn't want to scare off this *Boy*

Meets World heartthrob by being too forward. Okay, maybe that was something her character, Sarah Reeves in *Party of Five,* would do. But tonight there was no script she could follow—she would just have to follow her heart instead. Which, by the way, felt like it might burst.

"I'm a hopeless romantic," she once told a reporter. "I still believe in the whole Prince Charming thing."

Jennifer spent days on pins and needles, mulling the situation over in her mind. And then she did what she knew she should have done from the start.

"I decided to follow my heart."

For Jennifer Love Hewitt, at the tender age of nineteen, following her heart has resulted in a career that would be the envy of performers twice her age. When fans get together to discuss their new Hollywood faves, she is inevitably mentioned in the same breath as Neve Campbell and Sarah Michelle Gellar. But Love, ever the realist, laughed at the notion that anybody would compare her with her good friends Neve and Sarah.

"I'm cute sexy but I'm not an overtly sexy person," she recently told an interviewer. "I'm one of those people that if it came down to comparing me to Marilyn Monroe or Gidget, I'd always be Gidget. Sometimes I wish I was a little bit more like that but I'm not and that's fine."

Of course, several thousand fans might disagree with her.

But unlike many of her sexier acting peers, Jennifer Love Hewitt has made the grade based solely on her talent and a dedication to making her dreams come true.

"I'm constantly happy and excited about what I get to do," she once explained to a group of fans in a computer online chat. "It's like a dream for me, a dream I keep thinking somebody is going to wake me up from. For me, it's all about happiness. The happiness that comes from turning your dreams into goals and then achieving them."

Love has turned those dreams and goals into appearances in nine films, including starring roles in *Can't Hardly Wait* and this year's sequel to *I Know What You Did Last Summer*. Her considerable singing and songwriting skills have resulted in three international best-selling albums. And then of course there's the icing on the cake: her continuing presence as the adorable Sarah Reeves on the smash television series, *Party of Five*.

Given these accomplishments, it would not be a surprise to find an immense ego behind her sparkling brown eyes. The surprise is that Jennifer Love Hewitt, whose long brown shoulder-length hair acts as the perfect topping to her five-foot-two-inch frame, is alternately soft-spoken and giggly and down-to-earth. She loves mushroom pizza and ice-cold Pepsi and as might be expected, kissing. In fact, she has had so much spin-the-bottle experience that she's devised her own rating system, based on the number of bells that go off during a kiss.

"A ding is okay," she once laughingly explained. "Ding-ding is better and ding-ding-ding is even better. A really good kisser is *dong*! Scott Wolf [the love of her life on *Party of Five*] is definitely a three-dong kisser."

When not indulging in teen passions, Hewitt (or Love, as she's known to close friends) remains fully aware of the success in her life, but though she is the perfect role model for anyone who wants to be rich 'n famous, she still manages to define the girl next door for the nineties. She is more at home talking about boys, clothes, and parties than show biz gossip, box-office figures, and television ratings.

"I'm incredibly ambitious," she revealed to a writer. "I don't think I'd be able to make it as an actress if I didn't have drive and ambition. But the definition of success for me is personal happiness. I've busted my butt for something I've wanted so badly and the satisfaction of having achieved it is what has made me happy, fulfilled, and satisfied."

Hewitt isn't just ego-tripping here. You would be

hard-pressed to find anybody in Hollywood who would dispute the fact that Jennifer is unaffected by stardom. One of her earliest supporters was director Jim Wynorski. Wynorski, who directed the then twelve-year-old Hewitt in her first movie appearances, *Munchie* and *Little Miss Millions,* only told us what we already knew when he recently said, "Yeah, she's hot stuff right now.

"And the great thing is that she's doing such a great job handling stardom," he continued. "She has such a levelheaded outlook. She's just going through life and having a good time."

Love has a hard time looking at the celebrity side of her without a grain of salt. She does not see herself as "a celebrity," "famous," or as "being a star." In fact, to her way of thinking, her career is like a new toy. That's a good thing, right?

"It's like your mom comes up to you one day, hands you a toy, and says, 'This is a great toy. But if you throw it around and abuse it, this toy is going to be taken away from you.' That toy and my career are the same thing. If I take care of myself and keep myself grounded and keep a positive attitude, then I'll be able to keep that toy. So it is a good thing."

Jamie Lee Curtis, with whom Jennifer costarred in the 1986 movie *House Arrest,* has also gone on record as a big supporter. "She is talented, beauti-

LOVE STORY

ful, and sings like an angel. She has the tools to do whatever she wants to do."

In 1996, *Party of Five* cocreator/executive producer Christopher Keyser also sung Love's praises. "Love has a seventeen-year-old personality and a grown-up's professional perspective. You can't imagine that someone who's seventeen can be so professional."

And like any professional, she's not willing to rest on her laurels. Early reports from the set of *Can't Hardly Wait* were that Hewitt, while still playing a teen, was showing signs of maturity in her performance and drawing praise from her director and fellow actors. Hewitt typically has dismissed such praise in an evenhanded assessment of her progress.

"I used to make goals for things I wanted to accomplish and how I wanted to progress. The amazing thing is that my goals have gone 100 percent more than I wanted them to."

And she's done them her way. There has not been a hint of compromise in anything Jennifer has done and it goes without saying that she would not step over the line of certain rules she has set up for herself.

"I've always had a clear sense of what I will and will not do," she explained last year of her positive attitude toward life. "I've turned down things that

Love Song

would have required nudity or sexual things. I don't drink. I don't smoke. I don't do that stuff, have never been around it, and it's never been offered to me. In fact, the big daring thing for me is to go to an R-rated movie. So I guess I would be considered an OK role model."

However, Jennifer's life has not been the complete Hollywood fantasy. It's just that she took her lumps at an early age. Growing up without a father for part of her life has left some emotional scars. Her schoolmates were often cruel to her for no other reason than that she was different. And like most teenagers, she has weathered the trauma of first love. You can be a successful Hollywood actress and still have the usual days from hell. And when Jennifer is stressed out, she usually winds up in the bathtub.

"I've become a big fan of bubble baths," she told a teen magazine of her way to beat the blues. "And then I have those little moments when I go 'Aaargh!' Sometimes I go into my room and scream into my pillow or play a song real loud or have a day when all I do is eat junk food."

Jennifer was resorting to the pillow, music, and food as she attempted to sort out her feelings about Will Friedle and what should be her next move. "Finally I decided it was the nineties and that calling him up and asking him out would be a very nineties thing to do."

Her hand shook as she punched in Will's number. Would she scare him away by being so bold? There was a loud click. Jennifer held her breath. Her heart skipped a beat when she realized it was Will's answering machine. But she had gone too far to back down now.

"Hi, Will, this is Jennifer. I had a great time the other night. I'd sure like to get together again real soon."

Jennifer hung up. "At that point I thought there was nothing wrong with a friend going out with a friend."

1
Love Walks In

Children were important in the lives of Tom and Pat Hewitt. So were their children's names. When Pat gave birth to the couple's first child, a boy, in 1970, a lot of thought and discussion went into coming up with the name Todd.

In 1978 Pat became pregnant with the couple's second child. At the time eight-year-old Todd had a crush on a little girl down the street called Jennifer and so Jennifer was his contribution. Pat's choice was equally emotional.

"My mother wanted to name me after her best friend in college, a beautiful blonde named Love," Hewitt once revealed of her mother's decision. "Love was like 5-11 with long blond hair, big blue eyes, freckles, and an hourglass figure. She was the most beautiful woman my mom had ever seen. My mom had said if she ever had a little girl, she would name her Love."

But Todd's insistence that his baby sister be named Jennifer finally wore his mother down and so a compromise of sorts was reached. "My brother told my mother that Love was kind of a weird name and that, when she grows up, she may want to have a normal name to fall back on. My mother said, 'Okay, since this is your idea, you pick the name.'"

And so, when the baby girl came into the world in a Waco, Texas, hospital on February 21, 1979, she was given the name Jennifer Love Hewitt.

The first six months of Jennifer Love Hewitt's life were stressful ones. Tom and Pat's marriage had never been perfect; full of all the emotional bumps and dips that even the most successful marriages endure. But their relationship had seemed secure enough for them to consider having this second child. And, during Pat's pregnancy Tom had been the kind, attentive husband and father she expected him to be. However, stresses were slowly but surely undermining their love and so, rather than strengthen it, the arrival of Jennifer Love Hewitt seemed to put additional pressures on the marriage and ultimately signaled its inevitable end. Six months after her birth, in September 1979, Love's parents divorced.

Love Walks In

But far from being distressed, Pat Hewitt was determined to start life anew. She packed up her family and located to the small town of Killeen, a town north of the city of Austin that was known for its friendly neighbors, laid-back attitudes, and a safe environment for kids. Pat quickly adjusted to single-mother status and resumed her occupation as a speech pathologist at nearby Belair Elementary School.

Small-town life seemed to agree with the young Hewitt children. Todd's outgoing personality quickly became the magnet that drew neighborhood kids to the Hewitt home. Love grew into a delightful, spirited toddler and seemed to project life from her brilliant smile. And rather than shy away from the attentions of friends and relatives, Love would instinctively gravitate toward being the center of attention.

Pat Hewitt recognized the spark in her daughter. She would beam proudly when the three-year-old daughter regularly enlivened family gatherings with impromptu song-and-dance numbers. "I thought everybody's little girl could do that," Jennifer's mother would recall in later years. "But I soon realized that Jennifer definitely had something special."

Having Jennifer and Todd to occupy her helped Pat deal with the limited personal options that a

LOVE STORY

divorced mother of two had in a town like Killeen. Eventually she met Tom Dunn, a hardworking ambitious local man whose spirit and temperament seemed, to Pat, the perfect match for husband and father. Theirs was a whirlwind romance that ended in marriage. Jennifer and Todd were a bit leery of this new person in their lives but soon warmed to the man they would come to call dad. Tom Dunn was of an entrepreneurial mind and opened up what would become a successful custom T-shirt printing business shortly after the wedding.

Any doubts Pat had concerning how much or how far she should encourage Jennifer's obvious talents disappeared when Jennifer turned four. The family had gone out to dinner at a local supper club that featured a singer and a piano player. The evening had been uneventful . . . until Pat turned around to discover that her daughter was gone. She immediately panicked. Suddenly she heard a tiny, familiar voice coming from an adjoining room.

There, she discovered Jennifer, perched on top of a piano, belting out a very good version of the song "Help Me Make It Through the Night" before an audience of surprised and appreciative diners. Pat started forward to put an end to this impromptu concert. But after a couple of steps she stopped. Pat was suddenly proud of her daughter. She let Love finish her performance. After completing her song,

Love Walks In

to an enthusiastic round of applause, Jennifer was scolded by her mother for her disappearing act. She was also, in a subtle, motherly way, encouraged for her bravery and emerging talents.

Pat Dunn saw the handwriting on the wall. Her daughter was going to be an entertainer. Jennifer's mother enrolled her in dance lessons, where she quickly excelled in tap, ballet, and jazz. Hewitt's extroverted nature and high level of coordination for a child so young immediately made her one of the classes' prized pupils and the teachers would regularly exclaim their surprise and excitement at Love's natural abilities.

By this time Jennifer had developed a mature sense of herself and, by age five, was convinced that she was going to be a performer when she grew up. "I was inspired by the TV series *Punky Brewster* and the actress Soleil Moon Frye," she remembered of those early years. "I saw this little girl my age on television and thought, 'Well I could do that, too.'"

At this relatively early age Love was enchanted by the idea of fantasy and romance. She gravitated toward romantic movies and would cry and sigh her way through them, even through the really cheesy ones. "I was totally inspired by the movie *Sixteen Candles*," she remarked to an interviewer, the memory still putting a dreamy expression on her face years later. "I can't tell you how many times I would stare out the window and dream about seeing the guy in the red Porsche waiting for me."

In the meantime the relationship that developed between Jennifer and her brother, Todd, seemed inevitable, given the eight-year difference between brother and sister. As a toddler, Jennifer would attempt to join in with Todd and his friends. Sometimes he welcomed her, but just as often he would run and tell Pat that Jennifer was bothering him. Jennifer, however, knew how to push his buttons and would often have him doubling over with laughter at her antics.

Love was enrolled at Belair Elementary School, where, through kindergarten and first grade, she was a bright, outgoing child who was attentive in class and made friends easily. During this period she continued to take dance lessons and added more formal singing instruction to her after-school curriculum. She was also encouraged by her mother to perform at every opportunity, which for six-year-olds in Killeen were limited, so Jennifer's performing debut was in a less-than-formal setting.

"The first time I really performed in front of a lot of people was at a livestock show," she often said, laughing at the memory. "There I was in the pig barn, singing Whitney Houston's 'The Greatest

Love of All.'" But she also beamed at the memory of "the standing ovation I received."

As it turned out, a talent scout was present at her singing debut. He encouraged Pat, telling her that her daughter had a lot of potential and that she might want to consider relocating to Los Angeles, where Jennifer could test the waters. Love's mother liked what she was hearing but felt, at the time, that Jennifer was too young for such a sudden change in her life. She also feared what rejection in Hollywood might do to her impressionable young daughter's psyche.

Pat Dunn chose to hold off for a while on what she felt would be an inevitable decision regarding Jennifer's future. In the meantime Love continued to perform at area livestock shows, local telethons, and school functions and, by all accounts, was impressing audiences with her talent and poise, which was far beyond her six-plus years. Her performances, as always, were greeted with applause and praise. Again the talent scouts would come around with suggestions and, in some cases, offers of representation.

Pat was beginning to waver but still managed to hold off on any decisions regarding a Hollywood career for her daughter. She felt, in her heart of hearts, that she would know when it was time to make the move.

LOVE STORY

A change Pat did decide to make was one that took Jennifer across town to the Nolanville Elementary School shortly after her daughter turned seven. Jennifer made the transition to a new school without missing a beat. And, from her earliest days at Nolanville, she projected an image that was almost too good to be true.

"She was just a regular, normal run-of-the-mill child," assured Nolanville assistant principal Pat Pate. "Jennifer was very outgoing and a very nice girl. I know she never got in trouble. I was in charge of discipline, so I would have known if she had. At least she never did anything that brought her to my office."

Jennifer's second-grade teacher, Freddie Harrell, reported that from the very first day she entered her classroom, "Jennifer just fit in right away."

Harrell, who had seen a lot of children come through her classroom over the years, remembered being shocked by the seven-year-old Hewitt's level of maturity. "She was always like a little lady. Her mannerisms and the way she carried herself is something you would not expect of a child that young."

Assistant principal Pate, during Jennifer's first year at Nolanville, would often spot crowds of children engaged in animated and elaborate play during recess. Inevitably Jennifer would be in the center of the action, and often leading it. "She wasn't shy," reflected Pate. "And she loved being the center of attention on the playground. You always knew when Love was there."

Harrell agreed that the precocious seven-year-old did like to be the center of attention. "I remember that Christmas, I took the class on a field trip to a nearby mall and she went into one of these stores that had this booth that would allow you to make a video. When we got back to school, I ran the video she had made. She was singing and doing this dance. That's when I first became aware of how talented she was. There was just this level of talent there that you just don't see in many seven-year-olds. It was the kind of thing you just don't forget."

Jennifer's teacher also saw the "good student, very conscientious" side of her. Harrell recollected that the little girl "was very strong in the area of language arts," always "did her homework," and always "had everything done on time.

"She was such a perfectionist," she continued. "I remember one day she forgot to bring a library book back and she got so upset that she started to cry. Jennifer was just the kind of student that any teacher would love to have."

But what her teacher did not realize at the time

was that Hewitt was experiencing an unusual degree of frustration.

"I got the feeling that I never really fit in when I was in Texas," she remembered in later years. "I would host, direct, and star in all these little plays at school and things and none of my friends really wanted to do it. I thought what I was doing was just the coolest thing a kid could do and I thought there was something wrong with them because they didn't want to."

During the summer months Jennifer, under her mother's guidance, continued to perform live. It seemed confidence had never been a problem for the young child, and combined with her growing prowess as a singer and dancer, it was plain that Jennifer Love Hewitt was already performing at a professional level.

She returned to Nolanville and the third grade the following fall and, to the practiced eye of her teacher Ginger Wells, continued to present the image of a well-adjusted little girl with the best kind of leadership qualities.

"You could tell by the way she interacted with people that she would one day be something special," said Wells. "She treated everybody well and it didn't matter who they were. Everybody was treated like they were her best friend. And she would always look out for the underdog."

Her teacher remembered that Jennifer was continuing "to be good at her studies." "She was easily one of the best readers I ever taught. She could make any story come alive. Oh, there was a period of about six weeks where she was not doing real well in math and had fallen off from her normal A level. You could tell she was upset about it and I tried to encourage her by saying, 'Love, when you make all of that money, you'd better know how to add it up.' She laughed and her math grade was just fine for the rest of the year."

Ms. Wells's third-grade class would often have study free hours and Jennifer, she related with obvious pleasure, often used the opportunity to entertain the class. "She would get up in front of the class and sing these country-and-western songs. And you could see that she was really good."

By this time Todd was a teenager and so the dynamic of the relationship with Love had changed. Her tomboy antics were now often ignored and Todd was quick to become impatient with her. And being a typical teenager, when he got impatient with his sister, his response was often to torment her. Love shuddered as she recalled one particularly freaky thing her brother did to her.

"My brother, Todd, played the ultimate trick on me when I was seven or eight. I was finally old enough to have a Halloween bash. We lived on five and a half acres of property and my mom had turned it into this real cool haunted forest. Well, that night, after the party, the doorbell rang and I went to get it. My brother was dressed as Jason from the *Friday the 13th* movies and he jumped in at me. I started screaming my head off and ran through the house crying. He scared me to death and I vowed that from now on I would never open a door on Halloween again."

Jennifer graduated from the third grade in June 1988 and almost immediately found herself in the spotlight. She entered a beauty pageant sponsored by a local Texas organization and captured "The Living Doll" award for her talent, grace, and poise. By this time word of this little girl with big talent had spread throughout the state, and one day Pat Dunn received a telephone call from the representative from The Texas Show Team, the respected performance group that regularly toured the United States and the world.

Jennifer was being invited to join the group and perform on their upcoming tour of Russia and Denmark. Pat was torn about what to do. To accept would require her to go along and she was uncomfortable with the idea of leaving Tom and Todd behind. But she also realized that the offer was just too good to pass up.

The tour, which lasted a number of weeks, was an eye-opening experience for a number of reasons. Jennifer, whose life experiences had rarely gone beyond the Killeen city limits, was seeing new

Love Walks In

sights and interacting with new people whose existence she could have only imagined. The thunderous applause that greeted her performances were music to her ears and to those of her mother, who would watch from the wings, a smile permanently etched on her face, as her daughter brought down the house with intricate dance moves and a voice as smooth as silk.

Neither mother nor daughter said it during the tour. But, inside, both were feeling the same thing. Pat was thinking, "This is what my daughter should be doing with her life." For Jennifer it was simply "This is what I want to do."

Pat and Jennifer returned to Killeen shortly before Christmas 1988 and put their cards on the table. Pat had always found that dealing honestly with her children produced the best results and used that same approach in sounding out her daughter on her feelings about a show-business career. If only all parents were that cool!

Love in later years would remember the conversation well. "My mother told me, 'You know kids sometimes do things that they think they're going to be real good at, and if it doesn't go well, they grow up with all these awful psychological problems.' But I begged her to let me try. My mom knew she didn't have a choice and that she might as well say okay."

Days later Pat received a telephone call from a

local talent agent who had, on several occasions, encouraged her to make the moves necessary to take Jennifer's career to the next level. When the agent heard that Pat was now seriously considering a move to Los Angeles, he offered up the name of a reputable Hollywood agent who would be interested in talking to her once she relocated.

Another hard decision had to be made. Jennifer and her mother would be going out to Hollywood with very little money and even fewer prospects. Tom would be the only one bringing in money. To go to Hollywood would mean separating the family for who knew how long. Tom and Pat talked long and hard about what to do. There were tears and occasional raised voices as they struggled to make a decision. Todd was a senior in high school and it would not be fair to uproot him at this point. Finally Jennifer's parents agreed that if they didn't at least give Jennifer this shot, they'd be wondering for the rest of their lives if they'd done the right thing.

So on February 19, 1989, Pat, Jennifer, and Todd said a tearful good-bye to family and friends and left the small town of Killeen for what would turn out to be a long time.

No more livestock shows, telethons, or make-your-own-video booths. Next stop: Hollywood.

2
Lucky in Love

Jennifer Love Hewitt blew out the ten candles on her birthday cake. Pat and Todd wished her a happy birthday and gave her a hug. Earlier there had been a telephone call home to Tom for additional birthday wishes and to let those left behind in Killeen know that they had arrived safely. It had been a hectic day, and mother and daughter were too tired to do much more celebrating than that.

Pat, Jennifer, and Todd had arrived in Los Angeles around midday in an emotional state that had combined jet lag and unbridled excitement. Getting out of the airport had been a brief process, and after an equally brief cab ride Love, her brother, and her mother checked into their serviceable apartment in the Oakwood Gardens Apartment complex, a "halfway house" for aspiring child actors and their parents that is situated on a gently sloping hillside just around the corner from the HOLLYWOOD sign, and a short drive from most of the major movie and television studios. After unpacking, Love collapsed on a couch in front of the television with Todd while Pat made a phone call to confirm their appointment for the next day.

Mother and daughter went to bed early that night in preparation for an early start the next morning. Sightseeing would have been a perfect first-day activity under normal conditions. But Jennifer and Pat were on a mission. Before they had left Killeen, Pat boldly proclaimed that they would give themselves one month to gain a foothold in Hollywood. One month! One month to make it big in L.A. If not, they would return to Texas.

So there was no time to waste.

Pat and Jennifer met with the agent their Killeen contact had recommended the next day. Love was admittedly nervous but there was also an excitement that translated into a very real sense of enthusiasm that impressed the agent.

"I said I wanted to be a great star who can sing, act, dance, and do everything," Jennifer has often said of that first meeting. "But other than that, I just wanted to be a normal little girl."

The agent was won over by Jennifer's enthusiasm and sincerity, along with the fact that Pat did not come across as a potentially troublesome stage mother. Within a couple of days Jennifer signed on with the agent and began going out for her first auditions. This process was a new one for her and it is one she approached with some uneasiness.

"I hated the idea of auditioning," she said years later in looking back on those early days. "I never felt I would do as good a job in an audition as I would do in front of a camera with other actors."

Given her attitude, it came as no surprise that Jennifer was more than a little nervous the day she walked into the offices of the television show *Kids Incorporated* to audition for the role of Robin. *Kids Incorporated,* a show that featured preteens in a mixture of entertaining song-and-dance numbers and message-oriented skits, had been an immediate success since its beginning in 1983 and was presently going into its sixth season with an opening in its frontline cast. Love's agent echoed her mother's reassurance that rejection in auditions was nothing personal and that she should not get upset when she did not win every part she went up for. For the *Kids Incorporated* audition, this was particularly sage advice. Recurring roles for ten-year-olds were rare in Hollywood and so it was not too surprising that more than 1,100 child actors turned out to audition for the part of Robin.

Jennifer, by all accounts, turned in a quite naturally enthusiastic performance in front of the show's producers and casting agents. They were impressed with the believable sense of childlike innocence she projected, something that was often missing from more polished performers, and were amazed at her singing and dancing abilities. She received several callbacks and, within two weeks of her arrival in Hollywood, landed the role of Robin in *Kids Incorporated*.

Jennifer and Pat were immediately on the phone to Tom with the good news. Tom was thrilled at his stepdaughter's quick success in Hollywood and would later give a sigh of relief that it happened that soon. "It's tough in Hollywood," he said. "You need contacts or you can get eaten alive. Jennifer has a lot of talent but I also know she was extremely lucky." No kidding.

For Jennifer, her first job in Hollywood was a dream. With childlike enthusiasm, she marveled in interviews at the fact that her first break had come so easily. "It was my first job and it was kind of like a dream come true. I loved to sing and I loved to dance and I loved the idea of hanging out with people my own age. From that first day I knew it was going to be a lot of fun."

Jennifer and her mother had a special moment the morning she reported to the *Kids Incorporated*

Lucky in Love

set for the first time. After a nervously nibbled-at breakfast she suddenly turned to her mother and said "I would quit the business forever if it ever stopped being fun." Those words were music to her mother's ears. First and foremost, Pat had wanted what would be best for her daughter. But she would occasionally have doubts about whom she was doing this for. That Love's attitude was pragmatic and thoughtful made her extremely happy. Her mother smiled, gave Jennifer their "secret handshake" and hugged her tightly. It was Pat's way of agreeing with her daughter's wishes.

Kids Incorporated was a full-time job. When she was not at rehearsals or actually shooting the show, she would be in a child actors' professional school keeping up with her studies. As she had been back in Killeen, Love was diligent in keeping her grades up. Her teachers often acknowledged that she was quick to ask questions and always turned assignments in on time. When she was not on the set or in school, Love was finding additional opportunities to perform by appearing in television commercials, lots of them.

In less than a year, she had been signed to and appeared in commercials for Mattel, Inc., Circuit City, Ross Department Stores, Chex Cereal, and Mrs. Smith's Pies. In some of them her singing and dancing abilities were showcased. But in all of them Jennifer was all smiles, and a youthful, well-scrubbed enthusiasm leaped out to the camera. Jennifer Love Hewitt was a natural.

And that was good news to her parents.

Because Jennifer's success allowed the family to make an important decision. Tom sold the T-shirt business in Killeen and joined Pat, Love, and Todd in Hollywood in the fall of 1989. It was during a hiatus from *Kids Incorporated* in late '89 that Jennifer was offered an opportunity to join a group of singing and dancing kids who performed on a tour of U.S., European, and Asian trade shows extolling the virtues of L.A. Gear footwear and other products.

The L.A. Gear tour turned out to be a grueling as well as eye-opening experience for the now eleven-year-old Hewitt. The performers were required to do four thirty-minute song-and-dance performances each day and, under the supervision of a tutor, keep up with their studies. Jennifer and her mother did find time to go on sightseeing trips and as a result the world suddenly became a much bigger place to the young girl.

With the emphasis on *young*. Lost in the hustle and bustle of Hollywood was the fact that child actors were, in fact, children whose feelings could get easily hurt. It was soon after one L.A. Gear job that Love experienced her first failure. And it hurt.

Lucky in Love

She had gone up for a role in a movie and did not get it. It tore her to pieces. "I was close to telling my mom to call the airlines and was ready to return to Texas. But I had a long talk with my acting coach, who told me 'You have such a drive and love for what you do. Do you have any idea how miserable you will be if you don't do this?' The next day I was booked in another job and I got over it."

Jennifer returned to *Kids Incorporated* for its 1990 season and attempted to lead at least a partially normal life by enrolling in a regular junior-high school. As before, she excelled in academic life, with English continuing to be a strong subject. Unfortunately, Jennifer found that fitting in at a normal school was difficult and her teachers were a big reason for her discomfort.

"My teachers were really horrible to me," said Hewitt years later with more than a hint of disappointment in her voice. "They said I was ruining my life because I was acting and that I was going to end up stupid because I wasn't getting a good education. But the fact was I was learning much more through work than they could have ever taught me in school. It was frustrating to me. I had traveled the world, I had social skills, and I was an A student, but that didn't seem to make any difference to them."

Fitting in with her classmates was also tough.

LOVE STORY

Having grown up primarily in the entertainment world and around adults or other showbiz kids, Love exhibited a sense of maturity beyond her years and well beyond that of her classmates. This, she painfully recalled, made her an easy target.

Love had never been super popular in school. "When I was in junior-high school, the other kids thought I was a nerd. In their eyes I was weird because I acted, did things differently, and didn't go to parties. "Consequently she was picked on, teased, and just plain ignored." The kids just thought I was some kind of freak and would sometimes try to beat me up. I used to get soda poured on me and all kinds of awful things. Fitting in and being accepted was important to me but it was even more important to be myself. So I was able to deal with being picked on and ignored."

Jennifer was not being ignored on the set of *Kids Incorporated*. In fact, her relationships with the other members of the cast were as good as they could possibly be. Which was why there were no outward signs of jealousy when Love slowly but surely emerged as one of the central performers on the show and was regularly featured as the lead singer and dancer. One of her most enthusiastic supporters on the show was music director Reg Powell, who, early on, reported that "When I first

Lucky in Love

heard Love sing, I was blown away. She had a fantastic voice."

The majority of *Kids Incorporated* songs were simple, and largely forgettable, pop ballads designed to enhance a skit. But, in 1991, one song struck a surprising emotional chord. The song "Please Save Us the World" made an impassioned plea to save the environment. Jennifer was picked to sing the song on the show and the response was immediate. Letters and telephone calls praising the tune and Jennifer's performance of it sent her stock soaring. Later that year she took the song on the road, singing it, with other child and teen celebrities, at the Earth Summit, a conference on environmental issues, in Rio de Janeiro, Brazil.

Midway through her third season of *Kids Incorporated* it became evident that Love would not return for a fourth. Her experience and exposure on the show had caused her to grow, by age twelve, into a polished performer and the industry was starting to take notice. There were some moments of sadness and anxiety as Love prepared to leave the show for the last time. *Kids Incorporated* had been her cocoon for three years. Now she would be out in the world without a safety net. But Love's agent felt the time was right to begin fielding more diverse offers.

One of those came in 1991 when Hewitt was

chosen to sing, dance, and do aerobics in a Barbie workout video called *Dance! Workout with Barbie*. Filming the thirty-minute video was Jennifer's introduction to filmmaking, and while the drudgery of multiple takes and long hours was often boring, she was constantly enthusiastic and excited by the process. When not performing, she would wander around the set and look over the shoulders of the filmmakers. Hers was not the typical, fleeting childhood curiosity. Those on the set could sense that she was really interested. Love would get particularly upbeat when it was time for her to sing the exercise video's songs.

Which did not come as a surprise to those around her. At this point in her life Love fancied herself a singer and, to a lesser degree, a songwriter. In her private moments she often jotted down lines that she would fashion into tentative poems and song lyrics. These were creative expressions that only her parents and a few close friends ever saw but they were steering her in a direction in which she very much wanted to go.

Love left *Kids Incorporated* at the tail end of 1991 and, for the first time in three years, took some time off to relax and just be a normal kid. She would shop, hang out with friends, and savor the first moments of relaxation in a long time. But the vacation lasted only a few weeks before a telephone call from her agent presented her with a dream opportunity.

Jennifer's prowess as a singer had spread across the Atlantic and into the offices of Japan's Medlac Records. The label, which had a reputation for grooming pop stars for a primarily European and Asian audience, knew she had the singing skills and, with the right songs, could become an overnight sensation. Love was excited, nervous, and back to excited by the time she entered the recording studio in 1992 to record the album *Love Songs*.

Several songwriters, including pop star Debbie Gibson, contributed ballads and dance numbers, such as "Dancing Queen," "Bedtime Stories," and "I'll Find You." Love hesitantly brought her handful of compositions to the album's producer. She was thrilled when he liked much of what she offered and encouraged her to get involved in the songwriting for the album and she enthusiastically jumped into what would be the cowriting of the song "90's Kids." Also on the song list was the *Kids Incorporated* anthem "Please Save Us the World."

The long days recording the material that would become *Love Songs* were a true test for Love. Sitting on a tall stool as she sang into an overhead microphone, headphones clamped to her head, Jennifer endured countless run-throughs of the songs. She would wince and giggle when she hit a wrong note or forgot a lyric. When the producer gave a thumbs-up for a take successfully completed, she would let out a shout of triumph that would have the producer and engineers doubling over in laughter. For the most part, this little girl was coming across as the consummate pro. But the first time Love heard her voice, backed by a bouncy pop-rock accompaniment, coming out of speakers during a listening party for the finished album, she was once again the giggly little girl.

Love Songs was released in Europe and Asia in 1992. The first single off the album, "Dance with Me," rocketed to the top of the Japanese singles charts and stayed there for four weeks. Singles off the album also hit the charts in England, Germany, Austria, and Switzerland. Love went to Japan on a promotional tour in support of the album and performed in a series of enthusiastically received concerts in which kids no older than her screamed and applauded their approval.

"It was amazing, really cool!" she recalled for journalists of her first experience with pop-music stardom. "I had a great time performing in Japan. I felt like I was sort of in my own little world. I was as tall as everyone in the country. It was just so cool!"

Jennifer returned to the States and began looking for her first movie. After going through a number of

Lucky in Love

scripts, she decided on a low-budget comedy called *Munchie,* a very *Gremlins*-like story of a centuries-old creature that fights schoolyard bullies and unites preteen friends in their first meaningful relationship. *Munchie* made no pretense of being anything more than mindless escape but that did not stop director-writer Jim Wynorski's office from filling up with child actors vying for the role of Andrea, a young girl experiencing preteen love for the first time.

"The competition was pretty stiff," said the director, reflecting on the audition. "The girl who ended up being in *Jurassic Park* appeared to be the front-runner for the part until I saw Love. She just stood out. I could see from her reading that she was very lively and very inspired. She would literally bounce up and down as she was reading scenes from the script. Love just had this unbelievable willingness to perform. And a big plus for her was the fact that she had the skills to improvise."

Munchie was to be shot on a spartan eighteen-day schedule. Given the limitations of time and budget, Love was being thrust into a lightning-fast shooting schedule that would not allow her the luxury of more than a handful of takes for each scene. Behind the scenes there was some concern that she might have bitten off more than she could chew for her very first film role. Wynorksi knew very well the potential for problems as the first day of filming on *Munchie* drew closer.

"When you're dealing with children, you usually end up with one of two types," he explained. "You have the type that does a good interview and gets better on the set or they do a good interview because they've been coached very well and then they just die out when they get on the set. But I knew Jennifer would only get better."

The perceptive director also noticed that Pat Dunn was not coming across as the typical stage mother. "She wasn't pushy and she wasn't hovering. But she was around if she was needed. After all, Jennifer was still just a little girl. No, Pat wasn't a stage mother but I could tell that she was a wonderful mother to her little lady."

The *Munchie* story line did not require Love to compete with any special effects, but in her role as the love interest in the secondary element of the story, Wynorski speculated that Jennifer had a tougher task. "Making human interaction believable can be tough for adult actors, let alone trying to get that kind of emotion out of a child. But she was definitely up to it and she handled it great."

And, he reported, she was not uncomfortable with the swift pace of the shoot. "We actually had a lot of time to go back and fix things that were not right. But, with Love, there really wasn't that much to fix. She was able to nail just about everything on a first or second take. She was able to project the necessary elements of being cute and spunky real well. It also helped that the whole cast just loved her and that she got along well with everybody."

Following the completion of *Munchie,* Love spread her wings in her first prime-time television pilot, *Running Wilde,* opposite future James Bond Pierce Brosnan. The one-hour pilot for NBC, which followed a globe-trotting reporter who gets personally involved in his stories, was, by all reports, a good working experience for Jennifer, whose character allowed her to portray a wide array of emotions. Unfortunately, the powers that be at the television studio did not think much of *Running Wilde.* The pilot did not air and the show never became a series.

In the meantime *Munchie* was released to theaters. As expected, the reviews were mixed but all cited Hewitt's talents and maturity in what the critics considered a clichéd role. That she was so good in the film was not lost on Wynorski, who was considering doing another kids-oriented film.

"She was so good in *Munchie* that I felt that if I was going to do another kids' film, I would write the film specifically for her. I decided to write *Little Miss Millions* as a heavy drama that would give her a lot to do. I had such a good time writing it that I

LOVE STORY

decided to just call Love straightaway and offer her the part."

The *Little Miss Millions* story follows the adventures of a wealthy nine-year-old named Heather Lofton, who, with the aid of a reporter, attempts to find her real mother while hiding from her money-grubbing stepmother. Wynorski presented the finished script to Jennifer and her mother. At this point Love's agent and mother were keenly aware of her maturing image and did not necessarily want Love, who was about to turn thirteen, to get stereotyped in child roles.

"Love and her mother were cautious," reflected Wynorski. "But they read the script and loved the role and so Love agreed to do it."

The twenty-day shoot on *Little Miss Millions* was a literal mirror image of the *Munchie* experience. Wynorski recalled Love as being particularly skillful at projecting the emotions of sadness and childlike hope. Adding to the good times on the set was the fact that Love's mother appeared in the film in a small scene, playing the secretary to a bail bondsman. "In the few months between *Munchie* and *Little Miss Millions,* I could see that Love had grown as an actress. She was capable of so much more and, like before, she was a joy to work with."

By the end of 1992 Jennifer Love Hewitt's star was definitely on the rise. Her agent's telephone was ringing off the hook with offers. Love was turning into one of those classic Hollywood success stories.

"It happens that way a lot," said Wynorski of Love's career leap. "She had not done much and then, all of a sudden, she just snowballed."

3
Love on the Small Screen

Jennifer Love Hewitt turned thirteen in 1993. It was a time of change, both personal and professional. Despite her diminutive size, her agent felt now was the time to leave children's roles behind and concentrate on going after substantial teenage parts, so Love was looking for something more mature. Consequently, the time between parts began to lengthen.

At this time Love also began having her first teenage crushes. Like everyone, she would occasionally suffer a broken heart; love's never easy, even when it's your middle name. And, in typical Love fashion, she would react to the failure of puppy love in dramatic fashion.

"You can't breathe, your eyes are pouring a

thousand tears a second, and you can't see going on in the love department because you never want to feel that way again," she once said of her reaction to heartbreak. "A broken heart feels like the worst thing in the whole world. But, in the end, it really helps you to decide what you want and don't want. You learn a lot from a broken heart."

Hand in hand with her crushes was her growing knowledge of her body and how it was developing. "I guess physically I was maturing kind of early," she told a magazine interviewer without a hint of embarrassment. "I woke up one day and thought 'T-shirs will never be the same for me.' It took a couple of years for me to get used to what was going on with my body."

Jennifer was also having to deal with the increasing demands on her time. New photos had to be shot only a year after her last batch because she now looked completely different. There were the inevitable, and to Love, still annoying auditions. With her hormones going in every possible direction, there were days when she felt like the world was closing in. On those days she would invariably find her way to the kitchen freezer, eat a whole quart of ice cream . . .

And turn to her mom.

While her relationship with her stepfather continued to be a positive one, the bond between

Jennifer and Pat was the comfort zone that she would return to when things got too hectic.

"Most people want to be separated from their moms, but I don't," Love once revealed of their special relationship. "I need my mom too much. It's great to be able to come home from work each day and get a big mom hug and my favorite meals. I like it when she's on the set with me and I have someone to talk to in my dressing room and to hang out with. My mother is one of my role models and I've always felt I could go to her with any problems."

For Pat, her daughter's increasing success was forcing her to consider a change in lifestyle. Since their arrival in Hollywood, Love's mother had worked sporadically as a speech pathologist. But she finally made the decision, in 1993, to give up her work to devote all her time and energy to her daughter and her career. Initially, Love felt guilty about her mother's decision but she was grateful to have her mother around, taking a big part of the weight off her shoulders.

"She works really hard to make sure I'm taken care of," said Hewitt at that time. "If there are phone calls I can't make, she helps me out with those. But the best part is the idea that I have my best friend and confidante with me all the time."

Jennifer's brother, Todd, who was viewing his

sister's career from a distance, saw his mother's decision to give up her work and devote herself to his sister's as an important move. Love was at an age when Hollywood's influence could have sent her off into less-than-desirable patterns of behavior. It would not have been the first time a girl Love's age stepped off on the wrong foot, something that was not likely to happen with Pat's steady involvement. "Mom is a big reason why Love is who she is today," stated Todd.

Little Miss Millions was released to video in '93 to generally favorable reviews for Love. To many critical eyes, her sweet, innocent, and vulnerable portrayal of the heroine was the film's high point and once again pointed toward Love's potential to develop into an awesome actress.

The producers of a new television series called *Shaky Ground* saw that potential and signed Love on to play super-smart Bernadette Moody, the daughter of a white-collar father whose everyday frustrations provided the comedy for this primetime sitcom. Love liked the premise of the show, the fact that she would be working opposite an established actor like Matt Frewer, and that she would be able to add a glib, smart-alecky character to her roster of parts. Love, emotionally, was also at a point in her life where she felt she needed some consistency and balance and so *Shaky Ground,* with a guarantee of a year's work, was just what the doctor ordered.

Love adjusted quickly to the demands of making a prime-time television series. She was a quick study and earned raves from the show's regulars with her knack of nailing a laugh-inducing one-liner and projecting a wise-beyond-her-years attitude. *Shaky Ground* premiered in September 1993 in an almost impossible time slot, Sunday evening opposite long-standing television powerhouse *60 Minutes*. And while the reviews were decent, it quickly became evident that very few people were watching.

Love and the *Shaky Ground* company persisted in doing what they considered good work. At one point the show was switched to another night in an attempt to attract viewers. But it was a case of too little too late and *Shaky Ground* was canceled after seventeen episodes.

Love was disappointed. In typical JLH fashion, she became quite close with her *Shaky Ground* costars and was, for the first time, experiencing the realities of a business that often included being told that you were suddenly out of work.

"I learned that just because I had a job and was somewhat successful didn't mean that I was anything more than a working actor," she told an interviewer. "I realized that at any time I could not get the next job and not be working for months and months. I wouldn't be a star. I would just be an out-of-work actor."

But there was little time to dwell on the disappointment because *Shaky Ground* inspired a slew of job offers for Love.

Sister Act had been a box-office smash for Whoopi Goldberg when it hit theaters in 1992. And so it was no surprise when a sequel, *Sister Act II: Back in the Habit,* was quickly put together. And the role of Margaret, a street-smart Catholic-school choir member, seemed tailor-made for Love. She jumped at the opportunity to be in a film opposite Goldberg, one of her longtime favorite personalities.

"I could see that there was a whole lot of things going on with this character," she said of Margaret. "She's the kind of girl who is afraid people won't like her if she's not pretty. So she cops a bad attitude until Whoopi's character wakes her up to what love is all about."

Coincidentally, Jim Wynorski was mounting a *Munchies* sequel at about that time, entitled *Munchies Strike Back,* and wanted to include Love in a cameo role as an acknowledgment of her contributions to the original. Love liked the idea of going back. "Unfortunately, there was a conflict with *Sister Act II* and so she couldn't work on the day I needed her. Realistically, I knew she couldn't blow off that movie for a day's work on mine and so I told her, 'Okay, no problem.' And that was it."

Sister Act II was the latest in a long line of eye-opening experiences for Love. This was a major-studio, big budget movie and she marveled at the number of people and equipment it took to film the picture. At first she was nervous and intimidated at the prospect of acting opposite Whoopi but was happy to find one of her favorite actresses to be kind, considerate, and patient in their scenes together. "Whoopi could always make me laugh," related Love of her time on the *Sister Act II* set.

Like the previous film, *Sister Act II: Back in the Habit* featured a three-ring circus of gospel song-and-dance numbers and Love occupied center stage for the hours and days it took to film that sequence. She was intent on the choreographer as he outlined the moves and on the vocal coach as he put the singers through their paces. Love stood speechless as the singers, many of them professionals in the gospel world, ran through their numbers. She reveled in the fact that she was in the middle of all this entertainment. For her, *Sister Act II: Back in the Habit* was magic.

And it was also a time when Love made an important personal and professional decision. Up to that point she had always been billed professionally

LOVE STORY

as Love Hewitt. Beginning with *Sister Act II: Back in the Habit,* she began going under her full given name of Jennifer Love Hewitt.

"I had never made a conscious decision to omit Jennifer from my name," she acknowledged years later. "Since I was a little kid, everyone had always called me Love and, for a long time, I just didn't think to put Jennifer at the beginning. But suddenly it just seemed like the right thing to do."

And the reason it suddenly seemed important was that Jennifer Love Hewitt, at the ripe old age of fourteen, was entering a more mature period in her life. *Sister Act II: Back in the Habit* showed her as fully capable of projecting a young-adult image. The days of childhood roles were over and nobody was more excited at the prospect of playing more fully developed characters than Jennifer.

While conscious of the fact that she was growing as an actress, Love seemed more intent on the elements of make-believe that were part and parcel of moviemaking. "Glamour is still the big thing for me," she explained. "I'm an actress but I'm also a girl and the girl likes to wear all the best clothes every day, have people make me up to be beautiful, and to be able to act out all these romantic story lines. Making movies for me is still like living in the middle of a dream."

"I have my mind set on a new target for my

Love on the Small Screen

career," she said with youthful enthusiasm. "I'd like to get the younger Meg Ryan–Sandra Bullock kind of romantic roles. I'd love to get those sweet roles, those great roles."

A role that was neither sweet nor great was her guest-starring appearance, as a dizzy girl named Jennifer Love Fefferman, in an episode of the television series *Boy Meets World*. It was fun to do but Jennifer recalled very little about the experience . . . except that one of the show's stars, Will Friedle, was kind of cute.

At this point Love was beginning to be tentative about television-series offers. *Sister Act II* had given her an idea of what the high end of the acting mountain could be like and the quick dismissal of *Shaky Ground* and the transient nature of guest shots on sitcoms was beginning to seem a bit too much like work. Consequently, while not dismissing all TV offers, she had reached a point in her career where she felt she could afford to be particular. The young actress was not quite clear about what she was looking for but she would often say, "I'll know it when I see it."

In 1994 she saw it in the offer of a costarring role in a new dramatic television series called *The Byrds of Paradise*. The show revolved around the high drama of Yale University professor Sam Byrd, who, in the aftermath of his wife's death during an

ATM robbery, decides to start life over as the headmaster of a tiny school on the island of Hawaii. What was in it for Love was the opportunity to play a typical teenager for the first time in the guise of Byrd's rebellious fifteen-year-old daughter, Franny.

And what was in the mind of Hewitt as she contemplated whether or not to do the role was whether she could convincingly play such an un-Love-like character.

"I saw the role as challenging because I had so little in common with her," reflected the actress at the prospect of playing Franny. "I mean Franny was so full of teen angst. She smoked, she yelled at people, and at one point she ends up driving her dad's car off a cliff. I was nowhere like what Franny was, so I wasn't sure I could make people believe me in the role."

But Love liked the challenge, and the opportunity to film for eight months in Hawaii did not hurt either. And so she accepted the part early in 1994.

From the moment she set foot on Hawaiian sand, Love knew she had made the right decision. She took a couple of days to sightsee and do fun things like learn to hula. But it was soon down to business and from that first day on *The Byrds of Paradise* set, Love turned out to be a pleasant surprise.

"She was one of the most loving, sweetest people I had ever known," recalled the show's cocreator

Charles Eglee. "But in her role she just came across as so angry and tempestuous. It was amazing to see the transformation."

Love agreed that playing Franny was opening up sides of her personality that she had never explored. "My character was just such a grown-up, smart person that I was learning a lot just by playing her. It was a definite growth period for me as an actress."

But while the emotional flaws of a teen were the core of her portrayal, one of the most emotionally trying moments on *The Byrds of Paradise* came the day Love received a script that indicated that Franny was about to get her first kiss. Jennifer remembered years later how scared she was the day she and her nineteen-year-old costar had to rehearse the smooch.

"The director came up to us and he said, 'Now it's supposed to look like you guys have been kissing for a while, so go in the bushes and practice.' Now, I had never kissed anybody before in my whole life and I was scared to death. So we went off behind some bushes to practice. And all the time we were rehearsing the kiss, my mom was standing right on the other side of the bushes."

The Byrds of Paradise premiered in March 1994 alongside another new series called *My So-Called Life,* which starred another new kid on the block,

Claire Danes. Both shows were immediate critical successes, with the words "beautifully written," "snappily acted," and "quality family drama" typical of the praise heaped on *The Byrds of Paradise*. Unfortunately, both shows also immediately ran into ratings problems and the network, by midseason, was faced with having to ax one of the shows in order to give the other a fighting chance. The network chose to cancel *The Byrds of Paradise*. As it turned out, *My So-Called Life* would also be canceled at the conclusion of its first season.

Love was disappointed at yet another of her television shows falling by the wayside but tended to look on the bright side as the plane carrying her and her mother back from Hawaii touched down at Los Angeles International Airport. "I had a great time in Hawaii and playing Franny resulted in my gaining a whole new perspective on life. I went there as a teenager who liked talking on the telephone and was into *New Kids on the Block*. I came back all grown up."

Love took a few days to get reacquainted with her stepfather and to just be a normal teen again. She slept late, played her radio loud, and wrote poetry. For a few days she scribbled down song lyrics and was seriously considering putting acting aside for a while to concentrate on her music.

During this period she did entertain a few auditions. One of them was a pilot for yet another television series, this one called *McKenna*. The show, which featured veteran actor Chad Everett and newcomer Eric Close, told the familiar story of a widower and his often-at-odds children who return to the woods of Oregon to open a wilderness outfitting business. Love liked the idea that the show would be filmed on location in Oregon and that it would be packed with action. What she was not overly thrilled with was the fact that the character she would be playing was almost a carbon copy of Franny in *The Byrds of Paradise*.

"I was another rebellious teen who had lost her mother," Hewitt said, laughing at the sudden stereotyping. "I was another teen angst character, going through tough times and yelling at my father."

Still she gave the audition her best shot before losing out to actress Vinessa Shaw. She did not stew too long, however, setting her sights on what she was convinced would be the next big thing. Which, in Love's case, meant a serious return to music. The overseas success of her first album had not been lost on U.S. record companies, who midway through 1994 began making serious overtures toward Love.

"I began writing songs and taking a look at songs from different producers," remembered Love. "I

LOVE STORY

felt it was time to give the music and my singing what it deserved."

A demo tape of new material and the previously released album eventually made its way to the offices of Atlantic Records, which signed Love to a recording contract late in 1994.

In the meantime *McKenna* began filming the pilot episode. From all reports, filming went well, but shortly after the show was picked up for a weekly series, the producers decided that Vinessa Shaw was not quite right for the role and that the runner-up in the audition process, Love, was a better choice.

Love was happily surprised. But cautious. The cancellation of *The Byrds of Paradise* and *Shaky Ground* had left her still a bit shell-shocked at the prospect of tackling another series.

And there was the initial rush of enthusiasm for her music. The deal with Atlantic Records did not necessitate her rushing out an album and the little girl in Love was excited at the possibility of doing such *McKenna* action as rock climbing and white-water rafting. And so, right around the time she turned fifteen, Jennifer found herself in the wilds of central Oregon and in the middle of the action that was *McKenna*.

Love's love for the great outdoors was rewarded with a daily panorama of wonderful sights and

Love flashes the smile that made her a star.

Photo by Kevin Winter/© 1996 by Celebrity Photo

Photo by Lisa O'Connor© 1996 by Celebrity Photo

Love with *Party of Five* castmate Neve Campbell at The Golden Globe Awards.

Photo by Greg De Guire/© 1989 by Celebrity Photo

Jennifer's star power shines through even at age eight.

Love celebrates her eighteenth birthday at Planet Hollywood.

Photo by Kevin Winter/© 1997 by Celebrity Photo

Love cuddles with boyfriend Will Friedel.

Photo by Kevin Winter/© 1997 by Celebrity Photo

Jennifer Love has "the look" of success at the premiere of *I Know What You Did Last Summer*.

Photo by Craig Skinner/© 1997 by Celebrity Photo

Jennifer Love Hewitt with her biggest fan, her mom, Pat.

Jennifer Love Hewitt with Joey Lawrence at the *It's My Party* premiere.

Love hits the cover of *Teen People* magazine.

Photo by Lisa O'Connor© 1994 by Celebrity Photo

Love can't help but look beautiful.

sounds. That she was more than up to the acting task went without question. The producers, directors, and fellow cast members were surprised on a daily basis at the maturity Love was exhibiting as a torn, angst-ridden teenager. And when she was not sulking or talking back to her TV dad, Love was proving fairly adept at doing many of her own stunts, getting bumped, bruised, and wet in the process.

Love's approach to acting had reached an enlightened state during the filming of *McKenna*. Prior to that show she would often admit that she did not have a clear picture of how she did what she did. But at that point it came to her.

"You ask yourself questions and don't stop asking them until you get answers. You have to be good at taking direction or you can't do well. On any typical day you're given twenty different directions in a scene by twenty different people. Then you have to put it all together and be the person you are going to be."

Unfortunately, her enthusiasm and the general good vibe on the *McKenna* set did not translate into a large viewing audience. By the time the second episode aired, there was already talk of the show getting a quick hook. Love had heard the rumors and, privately, panicked at the idea of yet another regular job going down the tubes. Within a matter of weeks the rumors became a reality and *McKenna* was canceled.

Love was in a blue mood as the plane carrying her back from Oregon for the final time prepared to touch down in Los Angeles. Her mind was racing over a wide map of emotions.

She knew, in her heart, that television shows get canceled all the time and that it was nothing personal. But as she stared out at the Los Angeles skyline rising up to meet her, there was also frustration in her thoughts. Three shows in three years was a lot to give, only to have nothing to show at the end of it. She laughed inwardly at the idea that she might be cursed or be a jinx. Love finally put those thoughts out of her mind at the first bounce of airplane wheels meeting the runway.

She quickly got back into the swing of things. Her agent had lined up a new round of auditions and there was the ongoing process of gathering songs and preparing arrangements for her upcoming album. Love was at her best when she was busy and so the smile soon returned to her face.

Always one to find the silver lining in the darkest of clouds, Love looked back on her last couple of roles and found them ironically therapeutic.

"All the time I was playing these teenage angst-ridden characters, I was going through a lot of the same kind of emotions for real. So when I was going through puberty, I was able to get all of that stuff out at work and so when I came home I was stress-free and real relaxed."

Love returned home after a particularly hectic day of auditions and errands. She clicked on her stereo and began to sing along as the music filled the house with a vibrant rhythm. Then it was off to the refrigerator for a snack. The last thing on her mind was more business but that little voice inside told her to check out the fax machine before sitting down in front of the television.

Sitting on the fax stand was a pile of script pages. At the top of the front page was the abbreviation "PO5." Love stared at it for a minute. She went over the abbreviation again and again in her mind.

"I thought 'What's "PO5"?' " She recalled of her confusion: "I didn't have a clue."

4
Love Joins the Party

The first season of *Party of Five* was a rollercoaster ride of massive proportions.

The admittedly nontraditional tale of the Salinger family, struggling to survive and stay together after an auto accident claims the lives of their parents, had been an immediate critical favorite but a loser in the ratings department. Yes, its cast of young, beautiful unknowns, which included teen heartthrobs-in-the-making Scott Wolf, Matthew Fox, and Neve Campbell, had become the darlings of fan magazines. And the stories were envelope-pushing exercises in demolishing the TV-teen sterotype. But those pluses did not stop the nervous corporate executives at Fox from considering canceling the show on several occasions.

Over the course of that first season there were time changes, day changes, awards, and massive write-in campaigns by fans. At the last possible moment the Fox network caved in to the pressure and renewed *Party of Five* for a second season despite its less-than-stellar ratings.

But during the hiatus there were some changes afoot. The first season had been concerned, to a large degree, with the way the Salinger family dealt with the grieving process of their parents' death. Episodes rarely strayed too far away from that core element of sadness and mourning. The second season, as determined by the show's creators Amy Lippman and Christopher Keyser, would begin to focus more on character relationships. That change, they reasoned, would necessitate the addition of new characters to the cast.

The most conspicuous change would be a love interest for Bailey named Sarah Reeves. Sarah, according to that character's backstory, is an old friend of Julia Salinger's. As the second season opens we discover that she has spent the previous summer working at the Salingers' restaurant and has developed a big-league crush on Bailey.

Love finally realized that "PO5" meant *Party of Five*. She was not totally unfamiliar with the show. She had seen a handful of first-season episodes but figured that the widely reported low ratings would kill the show and so did not think about it one way or the other.

"What I had seen was pretty good stuff," reflected Love. "I thought the stories were pretty heavy and I recognized Scott [Wolf] from the time he had done a guest shot on *Kids Incorporated* and thought he had grown up real cute."

But now she did take a close look at the script pages that outlined the preliminary character traits of Sarah Reeves. Her brow furrowed in concentration as she scanned the lines of dialogue and character description. Silently, she began to mouth Sarah's words. They felt right.

"I made an immediate connection with the character of Sarah. I was like 'Wow! This character talks exactly like me.' I knew how to play her instantly."

And a lot of that immediate feel for the character came from Love's impression that Sarah was not a teenage caricature. "She's a cool person. She's not the typical teenager they put on television who is obsessed with sex and partying. Sarah's in school, she's smart, and she has a good head on her shoulders. She's stupid sometimes and she can make mistakes. In other words she's human."

By this time Love had developed an instinctive feel for the audition process, and since she felt that Sarah was very much like her, she felt it would be to her advantage to show up for the *Party of Five* audition as if she had dressed for a trip to the mall. And so Love, in a T-shirt, jeans, and very little makeup, opened the door to the *Party of Five* audition room. . . .

And suddenly felt like she had made a big mistake.

"I walked in and there were twenty-five-year-old women in little tight dresses with lots of makeup and styled hair," she remembered, wincing. "They were all these beautiful, tall, model-looking women. And there I was in this little T-shirt and jeans, looking like about ten years old next to them."

In fact, the *Party of Five* producers, in their early story meetings, did see Sarah as somebody with brains but with a more sophisticated look. And so Lippman, Keyser, and Ken Topolsky definitely noticed when the totally underdressed Love walked into the room to begin her audition. Immediately, any preconceived notion of how Sarah Reeves should look went right out the window.

"I could see that she had incredible instincts and incredible talent," said Topolsky of that audition. "She took direction well and she was smart. You could see that she was a special actress."

Love left the audition secure in the knowledge that she had given it her best shot and that now it was out of her hands. Given her track record with television series, she was quietly optimistic at the

Love Joins the Party

prospect of joining *Party of Five* and, she reasoned, even if it did not happen, she was due to go into the recording studio in a matter of weeks on her next album and so it was not like she was going to be sitting home, feeling sorry for herself if she did not get the part. The phone rang a few days later.

"It was the producers of *Party of Five,* offering me the part." She giggled at the memory of that moment. "I just freaked out and ran around the house screaming."

Once she stopped screaming, Love became uncharacteristically nervous at the prospect of being the new kid in a cast who had been together a whole year. In the tight-knit world of child actors, she had occasionally run into Scott Wolf. But when it came to the others, she was feeling totally intimidated and so she spent a restless night, tossing and turning with a mixture of excitement and nerves, before reporting to the *Party of Five* set for the very first time.

"Being the new cast member was a bit weird," she recalled of the day her mother drove her through the studio gates. "I wasn't really nervous about seeing Scott again but I was worried about the rest of the cast. I was really in awe of them. I couldn't help but worry about being accepted and being like the third wheel and on the outside of a lot of stuff."

LOVE STORY

As expected, Scott Wolf was the first to welcome her to the *Party of Five* fold, greeting her with a big hug and introducing her around to the other cast members. Any fears Love had about being an outsider quickly vanished as Neve, Matthew, Lacey, and the others all took turns welcoming her to the show. Love was relieved.

From that first day they included her in their jokes and took the time to explain what the routine was on the set. "They made me feel real welcome. They had this routine where they began each day by giving each other hugs and they immediately included me in that." They made her feel so comfortable that she felt like she had been on the show the first season.

The first few episodes of *Party of Five*'s second season confirmed Love's suspicions that Sarah Reeves was going to be the atypical television teen. In the season opener, "Ready or Not," Sarah is introduced as somebody who is not going to let Bailey's grieving over the loss of Jill get in the way of her love for him. Things continue to heat up real fast and by the season's third episode, "Dearly Beloved," an emotionally charged Sarah confronts Bailey with "I'm in love with you, you jerk!"

The following week's show, "Have No Fear" has Sarah moving very emotionally into Bailey's life. But the lightning pace of Sarah and Bailey's

Love Joins the Party

romance hits a snag the next week as "Change Partners and Dance" finds Sarah throwing up her hands and ending the relationship when she realizes that Bailey is just using her as an emotional replacement for Jill.

Love was quick to pick up on what was shaping up as a complex relationship between Bailey and Sarah and the fact that her character was not going to wilt in the face of rejection.

"I think Sarah is the girl version of Bailey," she reflected not too long after she began *Party of Five*. "They're both very smart, quick, and witty and so that's going to make things interesting. In those early episodes she makes it clear that she's madly in love with him but he's still into mourning his parents and Jill and so he doesn't look at me that way. So I go to great lengths to show him that I love him but I keep getting the shaft. But Sarah is a strong woman. She knows how to walk away from him because he's not treating her right."

Love had been a part of ensemble casts in her previous television shows but she was particularly attuned to the chemistry that she saw unfold daily on *Party of Five*. "It's really great fun to be able to work with an ensemble cast and to do things with as many as five or six other actors on a regular basis," she recently stated. "It's like an ongoing workshop. Each person has their own unique style and it involves a lot of teamwork and imagination to make those styles work together."

Those early weeks of shooting on *Party of Five* were a physical and emotional marathon for Love. Because she was still under the age of eighteen and subject to union regulations, she could be on the set only a certain number of hours a day. Consequently, her scenes, which usually turned out to be heavy on the emotion, tended to be shot earlier in the day. And, of course, there were those breaks for on-set schooling.

"Some days it would get really insane," she said, chuckling. "I would be in this intense scene where I'm kissing Bailey and then, all of a sudden, I'd have to run off and study for a test."

That would have been a big enough load for most adults. But when not on the *Party of Five* set, Love would race to a nearby recording studio for some last-minute vocal work on her album, which was now due to be released in October 1995.

At times during this crazy schedule, Love admitted to being "just a little bit" tired. But those around her would marvel at the way she would get her second wind. During a typical day on the *Party of Five* set, cast and crew members knew when Love was around. . . . Because they could hear her. "I'm always singing before I film a scene," she

Love Joins the Party

once explained. "Singing tends to get me relaxed and ready for whatever I have to do."

The relationship between the rest of the cast and Love continued to be almost too good to be true. With Neve and Lacey, Love could always count on moments of gossip about music, the business, and, of course, boys. With Matthew and Scott it was pretty much more of the same.

"Everyone is so sweet," she has commented. "You would hope that they would be imperfect for like at least one second of the day. But they never are."

Predictably, Love became best buds with Scott Wolf. When she came in in the morning, he was always there with a hug, a "how are you doing?", and "you sure look nice today."

"Scott is particularly down-to-earth and fun," she explained one day when describing how "she gets to work with gorgeous guys." "We've come to be known as trouble on the *Party of Five* set because whatever scene we have to do together, we always end up laughing and so it takes all day to shoot."

The second season of *Party of Five* began airing September 27, 1995. The immediate response was good. Ratings were up slightly from the first season and the opinion was that taking the Salingers out of mourning and into outside relationships was a good idea. Fan response also indicated that audiences were intrigued by the character of Sarah and her budding relationship with Bailey.

Two weeks after the season premiere of *Party of Five,* Love's album, entitled *Let's Go Bang,* was released. The album, which Love described as "very fun and funky," was a mixture of pop and rhythm-and-blues songs like "Couldn't Find Another Man" and the Love-penned song "Free to Be a Woman." Despite the tendency of music critics to dismiss albums by TV or movie stars as questionable vanity projects, early reviews of *Let's Go Bang* cited Love's vocal skills and a high degree of professional polish on the admittedly lightweight music. Love, who appeared on the CD cover striking sultry poses while heavily made up, was excited by the album's acceptance. But also a bit disappointed.

"The album title was a mistake," she once said with a giggle, turning beet red at the inadvertent double meaning. "I loved the song and the 'bang' was a dance. It was supposed to be pretty innocent and fun. But because the album was not promoted that well and the title was not made clear to people, people thought I was some kind of perverted kid."

The *Party of Five* story lines continued to put Sarah and Bailey through the emotional wringer. In the episode "Where There's Smoke" Bailey gives his good friend Will permission to date Sarah but

Love Joins the Party

finds himself jealous when he sees them together. Sarah and Bailey admit that they still have feelings for each other in the episode "The Wedding" and show those feelings with a passionate kiss. "It's a gas!" Love laughed when reminded of that particular perk. "I'm getting paid to spend all day kissing this gorgeous older guy."

In the episode "Grand Delusions," Love faced one of her biggest acting challenges to date: dealing with the discovery that Sarah is, in fact, adopted and struggling, internally, with the fact that her world was suddenly not as certain as she had thought.

Love began to get her bearings midway through the season. She felt she had Sarah's rhythms and personality traits down to the point where the character, in her eyes, was coming alive. She was quick to give a lot of the credit to the show's writers. "None of this would be happening for me if it were not for the show's writers. They wrote me a great character in Sarah; somebody who has to deal with a lot but who makes it through and comes out okay."

It was during this period that Love began dealing with her fan mail. There had been some fan response as far back as *Kids Incorporated* and the overseas response to her first album had been flattering. But none of that could compare with the wide range of emotions expressed in the bags of letters that had come rolling in as the result of *Party of Five*.

"I get letters like 'I don't have enough money to pay my taxes. Will you pay them for me?'" She laughed when describing the fan mail she gets. "Guys write, 'You're the most beautiful girl I've ever seen.' I get a lot of letters that assume I'm an expert on family matters. After we did the adoption episode, I got quite a few letters from adopted kids who wrote some really personal things about how it felt to be adopted." Love also gets a lot of letters from kids having problems with their parents. "And that's kind of weird because they think I'm some kind of expert and I'm not. Then there's the people who write saying that Sarah's a bitch and she shouldn't be treating Bailey so badly and that kind of stuff. It's amazing."

Given her hectic schedule, Love could be forgiven for explaining, during this period, that her social life "was not very exciting." But all that changed early in 1996 when she had what she considered her first serious romance.

Joey Lawrence, like Love, had grown up in the business. He was a regular on the long-running TV show *Gimme a Break* throughout the 1980s and *Blossom* during a long run in the early nineties. One of the things that set Lawrence apart from the flood of teen heartthrobs was the fact that in real life he came across as a kind, decent, very real person.

And it was those qualities that attracted Love to him when the pair met and began dating.

Love has always remained closemouthed on exactly what the nature of their relationship was. When questioned, she has always been quick to say, "It was casual, nothing serious." But those who reported seeing the pair out and about and holding hands claimed that it looked pretty serious to them. Speculation on the nature of their relationship ran high in both the gossip columns and fan magazines. All this attention to something she considered nobody else's business was amusing to Love at first but eventually became annoying.

"People always tended to make such a big deal out of it," Love once observed. "I mean all we used to do is eat. During the time I went out with him I must have gained about thirteen pounds."

Love's feelings for Lawrence were, at least in the early stages of their relationship, much stronger than she was letting on. For it was while seeing Joey that Love did what she would later admit "was the most outrageous thing" she had ever done "because of a guy."

"I got on a plane and flew to where he was just to be with him for twenty-four hours. I had other things to do but I just dropped them because I wanted to go and be near him. He understood when I said I just had to come visit."

By all accounts, Love and Lawrence did not have a traumatic breakup. Both had busy professional lives and just eventually went their separate ways. When she talks about their relationship now, she cites a busy schedule and a mutual decision to keep things casual. But one need only look in Love's eyes at those moments to know that it had meant something more.

"The polite way of putting it is that the business got the better of our relationship," she has admitted with a sigh when asked. "The one thing that I'll always be grateful for is that I got to see a much different side of Joey than what most people think. If he were to call me and say he needed something, I'd be there in a heartbeat."

Love continued to find more than enough to occupy her time in 1996. In the midst of a short hiatus from *Party of Five*, MTV approached the fifteen-year-old actress to host a pair of teen-themed specials, *True Tales of a Teen Trauma* and *True Tales of a Teen Romance*. Far from being a mere talking head, Love showed a real feel for the subject matter and proved a sympathetic, believable host on both shows. She also used the time in New York to guest-VJ on segments of the MTV video

Love Joins the Party

programs. Then it was back to Los Angeles and more trauma on *Party of Five*.

Everywhere Love went, her mother would go as well. Pat Dunn never turned into the dreaded stage mother that many Hollywood insiders had expected as a result of her daughter's meteoric rise. She played the mother first and foremost and got involved in the business side of things only when she felt, again in a motherly way, that Love was being asked to do something that was against her nature.

Love was experiencing as normal a teenage life as Hollywood and her mother would allow. She had a curfew of ten P.M. during the week and had only recently gotten a learner's permit to drive. To her way of thinking, she had just enough freedom and did not balk at restrictions and the fact that her mother was being . . . well, a mother. "It's fine with me," said Love of her mother's supervision. "I don't want to have to worry about all the adult stuff, even though I guess you could say I'm an adult. Anyway, I like having my mom around. I still need my mom."

The hang-loose atmosphere on *Party of Five* made Love comfortable enough to occasionally let personal information out. One topic of conversation that would regularly have her gushing like a schoolgirl was Johnny Depp, who she was totally hot for and to whom she had actually written a fan letter. What Love did not know was that one of the lighting technicians was a personal friend of Depp's and had told him about the actress with the major crush on him. Depp was touched by Love's sincerity and decided to show up unannounced on the *Party of Five* set and say hi to her. Love cringed when she recalled the day Johnny Depp showed up.

"It was one of those days when I was dressed in sweats and wasn't wearing makeup. I looked hideous. I was in my trailer when all of a sudden I hear the wardrobe girl yell, 'Johnny Depp is standing right outside.' I looked out through the trailer window and sure enough he was there."

Love went into a total panic. She threw herself on the trailer floor and began screaming hysterically. "I just couldn't meet him looking so awful. So I ran right out the trailer, right past him, screaming at the top of my lungs, and locked myself in the makeup trailer until he left. I couldn't believe I acted that way. I was totally humiliated."

Things continued to get hot as *Party of Five* played out the last episodes of the second season. In "Before and After," Sarah and Bailey contemplate having sex for the first time. The on-again-off-again relationship between the two is definitely off again in the episode "Altered States," in which Sarah leads her rock-and-roll band into some mu-

Love Joins the Party

sical and visual changes that rub Bailey the wrong way. The season came to an electrifying two-hour finale with the episode "Spring Break" as Sarah is mugged and Bailey becomes obsessed with her safety. Sarah can't stand the idea of Bailey smothering her and they break up.

The end of the *Party of Five* season marked the conclusion of the most productive year in Love's career. She had experienced success as a singer and she had found herself "in an amazing television show playing an amazing character." As she hugged and kissed her *Party of Five* costars good-bye for the summer hiatus, she was convinced that she had taken an important next step in her career and that the best was yet to come.

"I feel like all of this busting my butt is finally starting to amount to something," she said at the end of the season. "It's all just getting better and better."

5
Love's in Love

Love was too revved up from being in the spotlight on *Party of Five* to simply take the summer off. She wanted to be busy. Well, she got her wish; what she would be during the summer of '96 was overworked.

Atlantic Records had been thrilled with the success of *Let's Go Bang* and, in particular, with how well the ballads off that album had done internationally and so they were anxious for a follow-up album for fall '96. Love liked the idea of her music being her sole occupation for the summer and immediately began the process of selecting songs from outside sources and smoothing out the rough edges on some of her own material. She was literally days away from going into the studio when her agent called. . . .

With an offer that was too good to pass up, the film *House Arrest*. *House Arrest* told the wacky tale of a typical upper-middle-class couple who decide that they've had enough and prepare their children for their divorce. Needless to say, their children are not thrilled at the announcement and, in a desperate attempt to keep their parents together, lock them in the basement of their home in the hopes that they will be able to work out their problems. Word gets around and soon every kid at the local high school is kidnapping their parents and locking them in the basement. The character that Love would play, Brooke Figler, is the stereotypical prettiest girl in school. But Love saw more in the *House Arrest* role than a cardboard cutout.

"I know where this girl is coming from," she declared after going over the script. "You don't ever set out to be the most beautiful, most popular girl in school. Other people make you that way. This girl probably had low self-esteem and so she sought out the three or four people who made her feel safe and comfortable. And that made her rude and conceited in a lot of people's eyes."

Love also liked the idea that she would be in a cast that included such topflight actors as Jamie Lee Curtis, Kevin Pollack, and Jennifer Tilly. "I was really looking forward to working with Jennifer Tilly," enthused Love of the actress playing her mom. "In the movie I was supposed to be embarrassed by Tilly, who plays my mom. But all I could think of was that I had a chance to act with Jennifer Tilly and I thought that was the coolest."

However, Love's enthusiasm for *House Arrest* was dampened by her agent's warning that "they were looking for somebody who was thirteen years old." But she was certain that she could still be convincing as a thirteen-year-old and convinced her agent that it was worth a shot. Not surprisingly, Love gave a wonderful reading and "they called me back." But with the expected concern.

"The producers said I looked too old," she once recalled with a chuckle. "They were afraid I might be a little too mature looking to play thirteen but they said come back. So I came back with a little makeup on and my hair in curls, which tends to make me look younger, and I dressed down. Once they realized that I could pass for thirteen, the role was mine."

Love's excitement lasted only until she realized that the scheduling of the recording sessions would coincide with the filming of *House Arrest*. It was time for one of those mother-and-daughter talks. Pat was candid in telling her daughter that she had bitten off quite a bit and wanted to know if she felt

LOVE STORY

up to burning the candle at both ends. Love felt she was. End of conversation.

Love would literally be on the run for the next three months. By day she would be on the various Southern California sets of *House Arrest*. As the sun went down she would jump in her mother's car and race to a far-flung corner of Los Angeles and a nondescript recording studio, where she began the slow, methodical process of laying down musical and vocal tracks. When *House Arrest*'s schedule shifted from days to nights, the process reversed itself. She was eating on the run and getting barely enough sleep to satisfy her sixteen-year-old body. Love was the first to admit that the only thing keeping her going was adrenaline.

"It was definitely tough," she remembered at the time. "It was the movie set and the recording studio and that was it."

But this was classic JLH; she was enthusiastic about all that she was learning. "The movie was an absolute blast! I got to work with great actors and to play a great character in an entertaining story. And the highlight for me was I got to sing a song, 'It's Good to Know I'm Alive,' which is going to be on my new album. I also got my second screen kiss."

In the studio, she found herself learning a lot more about the recording process, and since she was doing primarily ballads, Love found herself

Love's in Love

being pretty relaxed. She was happy with the way her voice was sounding.

Love survived the summer crunch and, by late July, had wrapped *House Arrest* and the lion's share of the album. With some time to kill before having to report back to *Party of Five,* nobody would have blamed Love if she just kicked back and spent the waning days of summer at the pool, the beach, or the mall. But Love had other ideas.

"I definitely want to keep going," she said at the time. "I'm having a great time doing all these things and I don't want to stop."

Love's professional profile could not have been higher. Whereas Neve Campbell had emerged as the actress to watch in the nineties, Love was quickly overtaking her in fan popularity and was showing signs of catapulting to the front of the pack. By contrast, her social life was definitely in the pits.

These days she rarely went out in a social situation and while she would occasionally ring up Joey Lawrence, that relationship had regressed to friendship only. Love was good-natured about discussing her personal life. "As far as a social life goes, mine isn't very exciting," she admitted with a chuckle during a round of press interviews for *House Arrest*.

Which was not to say that Love did not fantasize about romance. She did and she had definite ideas about what worked for her. "I'm not into the bad-boy thing," she once reflected. "I tend to like guys who are down-to-earth and sweet. I like guys who, when I'm with them, make me feel I'm in the safest place in the world. I think that's the way relationships should be."

Love never got down in the dumps about her love life. But that did not stop friends from feeling sorry for her and, quite often, trying to fix her up. Love, despite her "why not give it a chance?" attitude toward blind dates, usually said thanks but no thanks. However, one day a friend came to her with a fix-up offer that was too enticing to refuse.

"This friend told me, 'You're going to love this guy.'" She giggled at the memory. "He told me that this guy reminded him of a guy version of me. So I figured I just had to meet a guy version of myself."

You could have knocked Love over with a feather the night of her blind date when she opened the door and it was Will Friedle from *Boy Meets World*. "When we went out, we hit it off," she remembered of that first date. "Will kept bringing up the fact that he was three years older than I was. After the date, I said to myself, 'This was my prince.'" A few days after that initial date she was determined to put her feelings about Will to the test by calling him up and asking him on a date. She got

Love's in Love

his answering machine and left a cheerful message asking him out.

What Love did not discover until much later was that Will was actually in the house at the time and that "he had another girl in the house with him." When he did not respond in a few days, Love, disappointed but not devastated, wrote him off.

As it turned out, Will was surprised and flattered at Love's call. There was no macho resistance to the idea that Love wanted to see him again and had made the first move. But the time was not right for either of them. While not serious with anyone, Will was actively dating. And Love was continuing to hang on to the last shreds of her relationship with Joey.

As expected, Love's mother continued to counsel her daughter on the upside of taking some time off but ultimately left the decision up to her. Love let her agent know that she was looking for something she could do in a fairly short period of time and the result was the script for a light, romantic comedy called *Trojan War*.

Trojan War told the story of a shy high-school boy who is in love with a girl and who confides in his friend Leah about his feelings for the girl. What he fails to realize until a series of comic misadventures has ensued is that Leah is secretly in love with him.

LOVE STORY

"Leah is your classic closet romantic," she said of her *Trojan War* role. "And that's really me. I'm a real sap when it comes to that kind of thing."

Love was surprised and a little bit uneasy to discover that her costar in *Trojan War* was *Boy Meets World* star Will Friedle. She had not seen him since their date, and while her memories of her guest-starring role on *Boy Meets World* were vague, she couldn't forget the enthusiastic personality and engaging, sly sense of humor he had displayed during their date. It also did not hurt that he was still very cute. Love sensed that she was going to enjoy her time on *Trojan War*.

Her feelings about the movie and her costar turned out to be correct. *Trojan War* was a parade of laughs and site gags that revolved around a cute, sentimental story. And because they were in so many scenes together, it came as no surprise that Love and Will became good friends who, when not working, would just hang out together.

"I thought Will was the coolest guy." She sighed. "It seemed we had a lot in common and that we could end up being good friends. We were inseparable on the set. It was really fun."

Love was happy but cautious. She thought Will was a wonderful human being but she wasn't really looking at him in a romantic way because she was still kind of with Joey. "But when we did our first screen kiss, we were standing on the studio back lot and he just looked perfect in the moonlight and I just knew the kiss was going to be sweet. And we kissed and it was one of the most unbelievable kisses I ever had."

But there was little time to think in terms of friendship, let alone the possibility of romance, because with the completion of *Trojan War*, Will and Love went back to their own busy lives; Friedle back to *Boy Meets World* and Love to *Party of Five*.

Those first days on the *Party of Five* set, much like her summer, were crazed. There was the first story meetings, in which she marveled at the changes in Sarah Reeves's character. When not involved in shooting the first *Party* script, she was involved in a round of press interviews promoting the soon-to-be-released *House Arrest* and the fine-tuning of her new album, which was now scheduled for a fall release.

"It's sort of like a cross between Toni Braxton and Des'rée," explained Love of her new album, entitled *Jennifer Love Hewitt*. "I'm pretty excited about it but I don't want to get too excited because I really want it to do well. It's sort of on the mellow side, not as dance-tuney as the first one was."

For Love as Sarah, season three of *Party of Five* kicked off in high gear in the episode "Summer Fun, Summer Not," in which Sarah and Bailey

LOVE STORY

clash on a trip to Mexico. In "Deal with It," Sarah and Bailey's relationship is once again strained to the point of breaking when Bailey's new living arrangements make Sarah jealous. The episode ends with the couple in a rocky state but still hanging on, emotionally, by their fingers.

Love was, very early in the third season, overwhelmed by the amazing support and feedback she was getting from fans of the show and of her character. Sarah had, to many teens, become a role model. Love gave all the credit for her character's popularity to "the writers who continue to work their *Party of Five* magic." But in the face of the overwhelming fan response, she remained at a loss.

"The response to this show and my character has been so overwhelming, so amazing that it's really hard to believe," she gushed to reporters. "It's changed my life tremendously. I feel incredibly lucky to have been lucky enough to be on this show."

Love's album came out in September, just as *Party of Five* was receiving its highest opening-season ratings since its debut. The album received a lukewarm response in the United States but a mammoth one in Europe and Asia.

In the meantime, Love's feelings for Will had grown to the point where she decided to put her love on the line.

Love's in Love

"When I kissed Will on the set, my knees had gone weak," she reflected. "That had never happened to me before. Finally I just called Will up and said, 'So are you ever gonna ask me out? I've been waiting forever and I'm getting pretty sick of it.' So we went out for coffee."

Love and Will had come to terms with their feelings toward each other, and although it was unspoken, they had in the best sense of the word become a couple.

Their dates were simple things; a trip to McDonald's for lunch, a bike ride, a picnic, or just hours talking on the phone. When they were not working, they were almost always together and Love, despite her constant assertions that they were "just good friends and nothing more," was making it plain to close friends and trusted acquaintances that she was suddenly caught up in the idea of romance.

"Will is incredibly funny and he makes me laugh a lot," Love admitted during a candid conversation about her romantic life with the press. "He's very sweet. I mean one day he just sent me a bouquet of roses for no reason. How sweet is that? Boyfriend and girlfriend doesn't seem like the right thing to describe what's going on between us. We're best friends who also happen to be soul mates. He's my best friend in the entire world and we just get along so well. The boyfriend-girlfriend stuff is like an added bonus. He's just great and I just adore him!"

And as the days, weeks, and months went by, Love's feelings for Will grew stronger. "He's just so loving, giving, and incredibly funny. He's the closest thing to a living angel I've ever met."

And an angel, she gushed, who was also a friend. "I think it makes a difference," she admitted of the state of her love. "When you date a friend, you've already seen each other at your best, worst, ugliest, and cutest."

Love being in love appeared, according to those cast and crew members privy to her relationship, to increase the emotion and passion she put into Sarah's *Party of Five* relationship with Bailey. This was particularly evident in the two episodes, "Personal Demons" and "Not So Fast," in which Bailey's infidelity with his roommate puts his romantic entanglement with Sarah to yet another test.

There was fire in Love's eyes during the scenes in which she rages at Bailey for hurting her and prepares to leave him for good. And there was tight-lipped anger and tears of frustration as she pledged her love once again and Bailey weighed his feelings for her. Love was usually pretty good

Love's in Love

about slipping out of character once a scene was completed but there were those days, during the filming of those episodes, when the anxiety Sarah was experiencing hung around in the heart and soul of Love after the director yelled "cut."

The third season of *Party of Five* continued to be an emotional roller coaster for Sarah and by association Love. There was Bailey's slide into alcoholism to deal with and her growing jealousy over his interest in Callie. By the time the episode "Life's Too Short" rolled around, Sarah had grown weary of Bailey's antics and broken up with him again.

Emotionally and as an actress, Love was being tested at every turn, and while she craved the challenges *Party of Five* was offering her, she would occasionally joke that she would not mind an episode where absolutely nothing happened to Sarah. The writers and producers laughed at those comments and then continued to pile it on.

The more self-centered side of Sarah's personality came into play in the episode "Misery Loves Company" when she initially refuses to help Bailey with his alcohol problem but eventually becomes a driving force in convincing the Salinger family that Bailey does have a problem and, in the gut-wrenching episode "Intervention," is actively and tearfully involved in forcing Bailey to face his demons.

In the meantime Love was diligent in her schooling and was now within shouting distance of her high-school diploma. "I'm definitely thinking about going to college at some point," she announced when questioned about future plans. "But I think I'll take a couple of years off after I graduate and just go after all the acting things I can."

Love continued to crave her quiet time as well. She would regularly be found in the privacy of her room in the Burbank, California, condo she shared with her family, listening to music while jotting down words on a notepad that would eventually become poems or song lyrics. The sight of Love singing at the top of her lungs was often what greeted Pat as she walked by her daughter's door early in the morning.

And then there was Will. Their relationship was maturing into something very real and pure. Consequently, Love reveled in the small, trivial things that, in reality, were the important things to her. "We just play and have fun," she proclaimed some months into their relatiionship. "It's not anything really exciting. We go to McDonald's and eat Happy Meals and talk on the phone a lot."

What Love had discovered about Will was that he gave the best foot massages on the planet and

Love's in Love

was a very good cook. He was also big on the kind of surprises that make a young girl's heart melt. The two were out shopping one day when she spotted a toy oven in the window of a store. She wanted it real bad but Will, in a surprising lack of sentiment, talked her out of the purchase.

"I was really mad at him," recalled Love. "But later that day he just showed up at my door with the oven with a card that said 'You don't have to grow up.' That was typical of one of the little things he does that make me feel so special."

Love turned eighteen early in 1997. It was a joyous time for her. She had Will in her life and her career was in high gear. In the final *Party of Five* episodes the writers had put increased emphasis on the Sarah-Bailey relationship, and because of that Love was emerging as one of the breakout actors on the show.

There was increased demand on her free time, and when she could fit them in, she had made personal appearances on behalf of the Fox network, MTV, and the Hard Rock Café.

Love was weighing a number of summer options as she prepped for the final third-season episodes of *Party of Five*. She was particularly psyched for the just-arrived script of the season finale, "You Win Some, You Lose Some," in which Bailey and Sarah kiss as a prelude to an emotional parting of the ways. It was tough stuff, even by recent *Party of Five* standards, and Love was already looking ahead to what she perceived as even heavier stuff to come.

"I've talked to the writers a bit about what's going to happen next year," she recalled at the time, "and what I've been told is that Sarah is going to be doing a lot of growing up and changing. Bailey and Sarah are going to see a big change in their relationship and are going to go off and get involved with other people. I can't wait to see those scripts. It sounds real exciting."

Love was already in an energized state of mind the day she checked the mail that was piled up in the living room. There were bills, letters from organizations requesting the use of her name for a variety of charitable causes. Those things went to her mom and her agent. And, at the bottom of the pile, was a script-sized package. Love had been warned it was coming. She ripped open the package and stared at the title on the front page.

I KNOW WHAT YOU DID LAST SUMMER

Love's agent had piqued her interest on this particular project. The writer, Kevin Williamson, was the hot guy in town after scripting *Scream* and the buzz was that this script was even better. It was also rumored that the cast was being filled out with

Love's in Love

some of the hottest young actors and actresses in the business.

Love opened the script and began to read. Suddenly she shuddered.

Love was about to confront her fears.

6
Love on the Run

"I was scared to death." Love shuddered as she remembered the day she leafed through the opening pages of the *I Know What You Did Last Summer* script. For a moment she wondered whether she should close the script and forget the whole thing. But even while it was freaking her out she began to visualize herself in the midst of the truly horrifying tale and couldn't help but read on.

I Know What You Did Last Summer tells the story of four teens on the verge of graduating from high school who accidentally run over and kill a stranger after a night of wild partying. Rather than go to the police, they decide to dispose of the body and try to forget the whole thing. A year later they return to the town where the crime occurred and they find themselves being stalked by a mysterious figure with a murderous agenda all his own.

Love wanted to do the movie in the worst way. But her own fear was stopping her short. Going back to the day when her brother had scared her on Halloween, Love had an aversion to horror and the idea of being scared. She had steadfastly refused to ever see a horror film. She was the first one to turn on a light when entering a room. And over the years she had admitted to having nightmares centered around her encounters with unspeakable terrors. Bottom line, Love was scared to be scared.

But there was a lot in *I Know What You Did Last Summer* that had her wrestling with those fears. "The character I would be playing, Julie, had the most scenes and the most to do. I would be in every scene and there would be a lot of special moments. I was scared to death but I really wanted to do this."

And so she buried her concerns about possibly spending a lot of time running from a killer with a big fishhook and agreed to audition for the film. Director Jim Gillespie recalled Love's audition with admiration.

"I saw more than 150 people for the role of Julie. But I just knew Love was right for the role when she walked through the door. During her audition I could see that she was a really disciplined, professional actor. I had a real good gut feeling about her, so I cast her almost immediately."

When Love was told she had the part, she decided that it would be in her best interest to finally see some horror films. "I decided I'd better watch some so that I could figure out what they were about and how they worked. So I went to the video store and rented *The Shining, Friday the 13th, In the Mouth of Madness, Scream,* and a whole bunch of other things. I spent a lot of time hiding my eyes and screaming while I was watching them but I learned how a character like Julie reacts in these kinds of films."

Love quickly discovered that a lot of what she was watching was nowhere near as complex as the character of Julie. "Julie's personality is something different in just about every scene. She starts off as this all-American girl whose future is hers for the taking. Suddenly she goes from being very strong to very weak and totally demolished. But by the end she goes from being scared and vulnerable to strong again. That did not happen in the horror films I watched."

In preparation for the film, Love also sought the advice of *Party of Five* costar Neve Campbell, who had recently gone through a similar terror experience in the film *Scream*. "Neve told me, 'You'll never be as tired as you're going to be on this film but you will also never have as much fun.'"

The film's cast was rounded out with Sarah Michelle Gellar, Freddie Prinze, Jr., and Ryan Phillippe. A week before filming began, the cast went to Wilmington, North Carolina, for a week of intense rehearsals. For Love, there was a slight attack of nerves as she walked into the rehearsal hall that first day. She was a big fan of Sarah and a regular viewer of *Buffy the Vampire Slayer*. And she had heard good things about Prinze and the others. But dealing with actors for the first time in a horror film was giving her butterflies.

Gellar and the others were thinking similar thoughts. It was the first time any of the actors had seen each other in action. But they came away from those rehearsals impressed with Love.

"I was familiar with Love's work and had been so in awe of her," recalled Gellar. "All the impressions I had of her turned out to be great during those rehearsals. She was just amazing. She was just so talented."

"Watching Love work was just magic," reflected Prinze. "She was there and she was very supportive to the other actors."

Director Gillespie continued to be impressed with Love's work ethic. "She was totally dedicated

Love on the Run

to finding the character of Julie. She was working real hard."

It was cold and threatening rain the first night of shooting on a dark, winding North Carolina road. Love and the other actors were gathered around a car, joking, making small talk, and trying to keep warm while Gillespie, amid a tangle of camera equipment, cables, and crew people, paced back and forth, lining up the shot. Approximately fifty yards behind the car lay the body of the man the car had just run over. The director called for action. Prinze recalled what happened next.

"We had to make our way from the car to the body," the actor reported of that dark and truly scary first night. "We all had to be freaked and Love had to just totally be in tears. It was amazing how she could turn it on and off. One minute we'd be joking and the next she'd be crying her eyes out. Jim [Gillespie] had this habit of saying 'bang on!' when a scene was cool to him and he was saying 'bang on' a whole lot that first night."

When she was not concentrating on bringing on the tears or screaming in a way that costar Gellar recalled as "being high-pitched and melodic," Love found herself experiencing a lot that was new over the three and a half months she spent making the film. For openers she was now eighteen, which meant she was not restricted to working children's hours.

"I thought my first job working adult hours would be in something small," she remembered of the many dark, cold, and long days and nights on *I Know What You Did Last Summer*. "But suddenly here I was on this film and working eighteen-hour days and I'm thinking, 'I want to be a minor! I want to go home!'"

As always, Love's mother had accompanied her to the film site and her presence helped her daughter deal with the sense of isolation and loneliness that would occasionally come over her. Not that such moments were regular visitors. The young actors had formed an immediate bond and would often while away the off-hours at nearby clubs and video arcades. In the latter activity, Love and Prinze had become particularly good buds.

But Love was missing Will. This was their first prolonged separation since the start of their relationship and nearly daily telephone conversations hardly made up for the fact that Love was truly missing him.

Happily, the long, complex shooting schedule left little time for her to be melancholy. As the strong leader of the group, Julie was in a constant state of "getting into makeup, getting my hair done, and running away from scary people." And, as she laughingly remembered, "getting a lot of bruises as a result of doing my own stunts."

Pat was initially a little uncomfortable with her daughter doing her own running, jumping, and falling, especially when she was regularly coming out of the stunt sequences with bumps, bruises, and nasty abrasions. But when she saw that Love was shrugging off the injuries with a smile and a joke, she quickly got into the spirit of her daughter's action-film debut.

"I did a lot of physical work," assessed Love of what she laughingly called "battle wounds." "I was getting beat up and hurt so many times but I felt they were kind of badges of honor and I deserved them. My mom really got into the spirit of things when she would rush up with a camera every time I hurt myself and take a picture of my bruises. By the time we were halfway through filming, I already had a whole album of photos of my injuries."

Love's character, Julie, continued to take a beating. She was required, by stages, to become an emotional wreck as her friends fall victim to the stalker with the hook. "I was spending an awful lot of time crying, screaming, and running away," she reflected, "and that got to be tough after a while."

For Love the worst part of doing this film was that the story line was so close to reality. "I would read something real scary in the script and then realize that something like this could actually happen. Trying to separate the truth from the fantasy had me scared a lot. But the upside has been that I get to be a tough chick and fight back."

Love was put to the ultimate physical and emotional test the night the film company set up shop on a nearby lake, where Julie squared off against the hook killer for a final time on a boat. The water was choppy that night and, at one point, the boat broke loose from its moorings and had to be retrieved. It was easily Love's toughest challenge and the full impact of her coming confrontation with her fear hit her as she prepared for what would be a long, wet, and cold night of horror action.

"I knew I was going to be on this boat with this psycho killer man," she remembered of that night. "I knew it was going to be tiring and I was scared to death. But I told myself it was also going to be fun and that this whole experience had been great and that got the adrenaline going again and I was fine."

As the last days of summer wound down, *I Know What You Did Last Summer* finished its last day of filming. Love hugged and kissed her new group of friends good-bye and hopped a plane for Los Angeles. She had a handful of days off before *Party of Five* was scheduled to start filming for the new season and she took full advantage of them.

She slept later than she had in months and actually found joy in going to sleep early. She and Will had a joyous, romantic reunion and were seemingly always in each other's arms in the following days. Love also used this rare time off to reflect on the past few years. And what she discovered was that she had been so busy for so long that she was, in a sense, not completely enjoying her success.

"My life and career is exciting, overwhelming, and very surreal at this point," she acknowledged of her nonstop pace. "There is not a real downside to it all except finding the time to sleep and to come down from it all. Sometimes I think I'm taking it all for granted because I'm always going. I wish I had time for it all to set in and to simply enjoy it more.

"I know I'm really thrilled with what I just did with *I Know What You Did Last Summer*," she offered. "It felt great and the thought of actually doing my first leading role had me close to tears a lot of times. I've always dreamed about what it was going to be like. The fact that it's finally happened is like 'Oh my God!'."

In those philosophical moments the now very grown-up Love was also finding time to think about where her career had gone and where it might or might not be going. "The fact is just now setting in that I have a movie coming out in October and people are actually going to see it. It's exciting and I couldn't be happier. If this is the last lead in a feature film that I ever get, then I had the time of my life. I do every job as if it is my last. But do I think this is my last? No way."

Love returned to *Party of Five* with a renewed sense of enthusiasm. Her cast mates were quick to notice the change in her. There was a sense of purpose in her stride as she walked across the soundstage. Confidence surrounded her enthusiastic tales of how she spent her summer vacation. It was obvious that Love had done a lot of growing up.

Another rite of passage occurred the day she walked down the aisle and accepted the diploma that announced her graduation from high school. In typical Love fashion, her coming of age was a Hollywood event, one that was chronicled by a camera crew from *People* magazine. "It was weird having a camera crew there. They were nice and didn't disrupt things but now I kind of wish I had done it a little bit differently. Maybe had things be more normal.

"I was eighteen years old and I suddenly felt on an equal plane with everybody," she said, looking back on the recent changes in her life. "Not being in school and being able to work adult hours with everybody for the first time made a big difference. It was great because I felt like a real part of the group. I was there when they got there and I was there when they left."

Love's third season on *Party of Five* kicked off as expected, with continued conflicts between Sarah and Bailey. She soon found that *I Know What You Did Last Summer* was paying creative dividends. The more defiant, self-reliant elements of Julie were creeping into her portrayal of Sarah and adding an element of mystery to a character that most fans of the show had felt they had figured out. When Sarah and Bailey raged at each other and she walked away, there was no guarantee that she was coming back this time.

"I could see that the writers had picked up on a lot of strengths in the character," explained Love of the new and improved Sarah. "She's a lot stronger and she's going through a lot of changes. Sarah is now an adult and I like the idea of playing her that way."

In the perception of the public, Love was also growing up. More and more magazines were starting to pick up on the fact that she was not only older but also quite attractive. She blushed at the mention of her physical beauty and tended to downplay her sudden appearances on magazine's most-attractive-celebrities lists.

LOVE STORY

"I get plenty of letters from guys who say things like 'You're the most beautiful girl I've ever seen,'" confessed Love at the time. "I read these things and my eyes just roll. I think, 'What? You need to look through some magazines because you're seriously lacking in comparisons.'"

Love has never seriously thought of herself as hot. But even she can't totally ignore the evidence: she allowed that she does have days "when I look at myself in the mirror and go, 'I think I look pretty darn good today.'

But as far as being a sex symbol . . . well, Love just didn't see it at all. In fact, she thought of herself as pretty average looking. "I'm flattered by the fan letters and the magazine best-looking lists I'm on. You can't be an actress and not be concerned about how you look. I can play around with hairstyles and makeup but I can't really change how I look because how I look is a big part of who I am."

And who Love had become by the beginning of her third season of *Party of Five* was a role model of massive proportions. She recalled one extreme example of her popularity: a series of appearances in which she was approached by very young girls who gushed that "they had changed their names on their birth certificates to Sarah."

"I can't believe the response I get," she reflected

after the encounter. "People are saying, 'Thank you for touching my life and my heart.' When somebody comes up to me and says, 'I absolutely love your work,' it feels very strange. But I love it because it makes all the hard work worth it. Being a role model for teenagers is just an amazing honor."

By the time the first episodes of the third season began airing, Love had pretty much grown into the idea of working adult hours. And rather than being exhausted at the end of a long day, she was finding herself with energy to spare. Which was why she jumped at the chance to moonlight in a small independent film called *Telling You*.

Directed by Robert De Franco, the film stars Rick Rossovich, Richard Libertini, Matt Lillard, and Peter Facinelli. It tells the story of a troubled young man who feels that when he cheated on his girlfriend in high school years earlier, he sent his life on a downhill slide. As *Telling You* unfolds, he comes across his old girlfriend and feels compelled to confess what he did. The reason Love jumped at the chance to do a smaller film than *I Know What You Did Last Summer* was that it would give her the opportunity to play a type of character she had been dying to play: a dumb one.

"I've always been kind of cast as the smart, spunky kid and I liked the idea that I would be playing a Long Island Lolita airhead in Deb Friedman, who was annoying and perky. I liked the idea that no one could stand this character and that she had no brain cells."

And so Love enthusiastically threw herself into a seemingly impossible work schedule. By day, she was the always-in-turmoil Sarah on the *Party of Five* set. Then, after a quick bite of supper and, when possible, a nap, she would magically transform into a very un-Sarah-like stereotype. Then it was rush back home and a couple of hours' sleep before returning to the *Party of Five* set.

Rather than suffer as the result of playing, simultaneously, two distinctly different characters, Love's performances were, if anything, sharper and more focused than anybody could have imagined. In Love's hands, Sarah was taking on more than the surface toughness she had exhibited before, while her character in *Telling You* benefited from her inexperience with that kind of role and came across, according to director De Franco and her costars, more substantial than one would expect from the cartoon nature of the character.

It had become obvious that movies would soon be calling on Love with some regularity and this led to the inevitable rumors that she would be leaving *Party of Five* at the conclusion of the current season. At one point the rumors were flying so hot and heavy that a spokesperson for Love went public with the statement that "She will continue on the show as long as her bosses want her." The producers of the show were quick to follow suit, saying that Love would be on *Party of Five* as long as she wanted to play Sarah.

As for Love, she was in no hurry to make that kind of career decision. "I like doing films and being able to change myself around all the time. But I want to keep being on *Party of Five*. My secret wish would be that *Party of Five* would be an ongoing series of motion pictures."

By this time Love's previous hilarious and humiliating encounter with Johnny Depp on the TV show's set had become the stuff of legend, resulting in many jokes made at Love's expense. People would remind her of the incident, and depending on her mood, Love would either laugh along with them or relive her embarrassment in gruesome detail. Finally an opportunity arose that allowed her to fulfill her dream of meeting the handsome actor.

Depp's new picture, *Donnie Brasco,* was about to open and the powers that be at the film's studio sent over a couple of premiere tickets to Love. That night, every bit the nervous teenager, she waited outside the theater for Depp's arrival. Finally her idol showd up.

"I called out to him as he was walking in," she

had remembered of that night. "He turned around, looked at me, and waved. It felt like it was slow motion."

Love had hung around outside for so long that her seats were given to somebody else and she was not allowed in the theater to see the movie. But she could have cared less at that point. She had something else in mind.

"While the movie was playing, I went to where a screening party was going to be held and went up to a security guard. I told him, 'This is the situation. I have to meet him.' The guard looked at me kind of funny for a minute, then smiled and took me into the party. Later I finally got to meet Johnny. He knew exactly who I was. My God! His voice just sounded like butter."

I Know What You Did Last Summer opened in October 1997 to rave reviews. Love was, likewise, applauded as an actress mature beyond her years who had succeeded in adding a new wrinkle to the well-worn image of horror heroine. The figures were barely in on the film's opening weekend when she and costar Prinze had signed on to do a sequel to be filmed during the late spring and early summer months of 1998.

As hectic as her schedule was, Love always managed to find quality time to be with Will. Their relationship, now a year and a half old, had defied the Hollywood odds and, in the public and media's eyes, taken that next inevitable step toward the question of marriage. Love would blush and laugh when asked about when her relationship with Will would turn permanent.

"We haven't discussed marriage," she said shortly after completing *Telling You*. "That's kind of a scary thing for us at this point. I mean I'm only eighteen and Will and I have a whole lot of life to live. It's not like I'm afraid of commitment," she continued candidly. "I've been making wedding plans since I was twelve years old and I read all the bridal magazines every month.

"It's just that for me, marriage is not something to be taken lightly. When you're eighteen years old, you have no idea if the person you're with is going to be somebody you're going to want to marry one day. At this point Will and I are just enjoying being in love and being happy. We're both a little too busy to be talking about that stuff."

And for Love, busy was about to become busier.

7
Love Unlimited

Love completed her third season on *Party of Five* on the highest of highs. And she was grateful.

"The one thing I've been really happy with is that, right now, there's a lot of really good roles for people my age," she said at the time. "The people in the industry are now seeing that somebody eighteen or nineteen years old can carry a film without having to fall back on teenage stereotypes."

Which is why, when looking around for a summer project, Love immediately latched onto *Can't Hardly Wait*. Very much in the tradition of such teen classics as *Pretty in Pink* and *The Breakfast Club*, *Can't Hardly Wait* focuses on a group of teenagers who have gone through four years of high school together and are about to attend their graduation party. They all have different reasons for going and Love, when sizing up the character of Amanda Beckett, found a number of reasons for saying yes to the part.

Love's character is the prom queen, the homecoming queen who has spent her entire high-school career trying to prove that she has a brain and that she's more than just Ms. Popular. "Amanda is the sort of girl you would picture Alanis Morissette as having been in high school. I also liked the idea that she did not know that she was the dream girl of another character who had finally screwed up the courage to tell her how he really felt."

The producers of *Can't Hardly Wait* were thrilled that Love was excited by the character. "She was the only person we went to for the role," enthused the film's executive producer Jenno Topping. "We were thrilled when she loved it and immediately said yes."

Can't Hardly Wait, which featured a cast of name actors like Love and on the rise people like Ethan Embry and Jerry O'Connell, was easily the loosest film set she had worked on. Yes, they were professional actors but it did not take much to send them into fits of laughter, and the practical jokes and all manner of teen high jinks often sent the film's director up a tree. "There was always somebody standing over in the corner when we were trying to get a scene done, who would do or say something that would crack everyone up," revealed Love of the *Can't Hardly Wait* cast's occasional bad behavior.

Can't Hardly Wait also proved to be a creative turning point of sorts for Love. Amanda, while still essentially a teenager, had been written as a character on the verge of adulthood and so, by turns, Love would have to reach into a grown-up state of mind. Those were magic moments for Love's mother and those on the set of *Can't Hardly Wait*.

Of course there were the expected nonmagical moments. During one particularly hectic day, a simple dialogue between Amanda and a character called Earth Girl went off seemingly flawless on the first take. But the director saw something he did not like and ordered another take . . . and another and another. After a dozen takes, the scene was finally wrapped to everyone's satisfaction. Love, reportedly dizzy from the repetition, took it in stride.

It's not always because it's bad or you didn't do the right thing," she speculated. "Sometimes it has to do with someone in the background moving a different way or they had to get my reaction in a close-up."

Later that day, Love, who had been up since 4 A.M. and had already put in a six-hour day, took a break inside her trailer. She got out of her "Amanda" clothes and slipped into a comfortable robe. It was at moments like this that Love admitted to bouts of loneliness and vulnerability. At one point she gazed around her trailer. Wherever she looked was a picture of Will. Tacking up pictures of her true love had been a good idea. It wasn't as good as having Will there with her, but it was the next best thing.

The conclusion of filming *Can't Hardly Wait* did not mean the party was over for Love. She immediately returned to *Party of Five* and another season as the emotionally charged Sarah. Love instinctively clicked into the character and those early-season stories reinforced the notion that both the character and the actress were in a period of growth. Sarah was still the tough single-minded girl but her reactions to the relationship with Bailey and, by association, with the Salingers and their world had taken on a more mature edge. Wisdom, rather than emotion, was becoming more of what made Sarah tick.

Love was thrilled with what was going on with *Party of Five* but, for the first time, she was finding herself distracted by other career choices. That she was becoming a star-celebrity with no small amount of clout was not lost on her agent. He suggested, and Love's mother agreed, that the eighteen-year-old set up her own production company and begin to think about creating her own film projects. Thus was born Daybreak Productions and Love began getting used to the idea of having the title "producer" in front of her name.

Music was also on her mind. Her last album had not been a smash but it had had respectable sales and she was encouraged by the fan response. She was anxious to get back into the recording studio, possibly even before the end of the year. But, as her acting obligations piled up, Love found that, for the first time, there was not enough time.

"I just don't have the time to give the music what it deserves." She sighed with more than a little disappointment in her voice. "I'm thinking about trying to go back into the studio in early '98 but I have the feeling that I'm going to need a lot more writing time."

Part of her creative conflict centered on the fact that she was scheduled to start filming *I Still Know What You Did Last Summer,* the sequel to *I Know What You Did Last Summer* right after *Party of Five* ended its current season. Locations in Los Angeles and Mexico had already been selected. A new cast, including teen singer-actress Brandy, was already in place and a capable director in Danny Cannon was on board. There was only one thing missing.

"They're frantically writing the script right now, so I don't have any idea what it's going to be about.

I can only hope that this one is as much of a blast as the first one was. But despite what happened to me at the end of the last film, I'll be back. I'll be in pain but I'll be back."

Love turned nineteen shortly after the new year with a raucous celebration that included family, friends, and, of course, Will. Love's love had been incredibly understanding about her insane work schedule. And that understanding was rewarded with just about all the free time she had. Bike riding had become a typical Love-Will kind of date when the weather was good. And they would often be spotted going into or coming out of a movie theater.

"Will has always been there for me," she cooed during this period. "He always makes me feel special."

Special turned out to be the watch word when Love finally reported to the set of *I Still Know What You Did Last Summer*. The finished script had succeeded in upping the thrills and chills and had painted Julie as a battle-scarred warrior in the war against the terrors of the night. Love and Prinze, having been down this road once before, assumed the unofficial role of leaders among the actors on the set, offering up suggestions on how to play fright scenes and regaling the newcomers with tales about the filming of the original feature. Love formed a particularly friendly bond with Brandy, whose career as an actress-singer had largely paralleled hers.

Once again Love was responsible for her own stunts and once again her mother was on hand, camera in hand, to begin filling up another album of Love's cuts and bruises.

But this time Love was better prepared for the fact that she would be doing her own stunts. For months prior to the beginning of shooting she had been involved in a "killer workout" that included weight training, aerobics, and a special protein diet. "I was pumped up and totally buffed," she chuckled at her Terminator-like condition for the role.

And it was a good thing, too, because *I Still Know What You Did Last Summer* had upped the action quotient and Love soon chalked up a total of thirty-eight bumps and bruises.

"Every time I turned around, we were doing some kind of fight scene," laughed Love. "And there was always blood flying everywhere. In fact, I still have blood under my fingernails."

Love completed *I Still Know What You Did Last Summer* just about the time *Can't Hardly Wait* opened in theaters. After everybody had flocked to see *Godzilla*—or not—there had been a noticeable downturn in the number of films aimed directly at a young-adult audience. *Can't Hardly Wait* filled the teen need perfectly and went on to become a

LOVE STORY

critical and box-office success. Love's portrayal of Amanda was singled out for particularly strong praise; citing her growth as an actress and, more importantly to Love, the fact that she had effectively navigated the minefield of stereotypic teen roles and was now ready to take on the adult world.

Which, in her mind, meant she was going to have to get serious about generating projects for her production company. Love had looked at a number of scripts and story ideas but had found nothing that interested her. Until the night she went to bed after a particularly busy day and had a dream.

"I dreamed about this story of a wedding planner who falls in love with the groom at one of her weddings. It was a strange dream, but when I woke up the next morning I thought it was a great idea for a movie."

Love immediately jotted down the outline for her dream, which she later titled *Cupid's Love*. In short order, her enthusiastic management team had taken the idea around Hollywood, letting studios know that the project was available with Love attached as actor and executive producer. Love had expected that her inexperience on the production side of the business would be a stumbling block to getting a deal.

Love reverted to Acting 101 as she prepared to meet the bottom-line studio executives. She put on a conservative business suit and wire-rimmed glasses (despite the fact that she does not normally wear glasses), in an attempt to present a more mature image.

"I'm an actress," chuckled Love as she prepared to meet the studio top dogs. "I know how to dress for the role and adopt the right attitude. I want to look serious so the studio people will take me seriously."

Love knew a deal for *Cupid's Love* was not going to be automatic despite her past successes, but was not prepared for a weeklong march through a number of Hollywood studios in an attempt to make her dream a reality.

"I went around for a week to all the studio executives in Los Angeles," she recalled. "It was incredibly nerve-wracking." But her persistence was rewarded when New Line Cinema and producer-director Betty Thomas agreed to take on *Cupid's Love* and immediately put the project into development. And sweetened the deal with a $500,000 check!

"I'm excited that a studio would take a concept I dreamed up but was also willing to put their faith in me as an actress and as a producer."

With the emphasis being on producer. "I would love to produce stuff. I really, really would. The only reason I wanted to do it in the first place is because I feel my part of the filmmaking is so small. I get to come in and do my part after everybody else has done theirs. They get to be there for the meetings and putting the characters together. I just get to play it after they're done. I want so badly to be a bigger part of the creative process."

But *Cupid's Love* was at the end of a suddenly very long line of movies that Love was either attached to or reportedly interested in. Shortly before she began filming *I Still Know What You Did Last Summer,* she did an informal read-through of a script entitled *Blood and Chocolate,* in which a female werewolf puts her life in jeopardy by falling in love with a human being. Love expressed some interest but, by that time, had already committed to a rock-and-roll comedy called *The Suburbans,* in which former teen rock stars and their families are dragged back into a nostalgic comeback by an eager young record-company executive.

Love reported to the *Suburbans* set shortly after completing *I Still Know What You Did Last Summer* and was relieved to discover that the nonstop horror of the previous film had been replaced by nonstop rock-and-roll laughs.

But it wasn't all work and no play for Love during the summer of '98. With Will, likewise, on hiatus from *Boy Meets World,* the loving couple were able to find quality time to be together.

Love Unlimited

Horseback riding became a new way for Love and Will to hang out and they would spend hours riding the trails in and around Los Angeles. Good weather often led them to the beach, where picnics and romps in the surf filled out days that often found them gazing dreamily out at the sun as it sank beneath the horizon.

As always, Will remained the committed romantic, doing and saying the small things that would instantly brighten up Love's life. A big reason for the longevity of their relationship was the fact that Will was not the jealous type. That Love's career seemed to be making bigger strides than his did not bother him in the least. Nor did the fact that her career had put her in close proximity to the likes of oh, say Johnny Depp. He was supportive of everything Love was doing and she was there for him.

"We're friends and we continued to be there for each other," gushed Love when describing their relationship. "He's just everything to me."

She was also finding time for solitary but no less important pursuits. Love could often be found sitting cross-legged on her bed or on the floor, writing letters to her small group of personal friends. Poetry had also become an ever-more-important creative outlet and Love spent hours scribbling down her most personal and intimate thoughts. And in a move to expand her musical horizons, she bought a guitar and began picking out simple chord patterns. She was soon accompanying herself on guitar in intimate rehearsals witnessed by a handful of family members and friends.

"I'm really kind of proud of my singing," she announced not too long after picking up the guitar. "The singing is something that comes from my soul and my gut. I love music so much, it would be a major disappointment if I couldn't carry a tune."

Life on the *Party of Five* set continued to be one big happy family. Neve and Love had always been close but now, with the success of *I Know What You Did Last Summer* and *Can't Hardly Wait*, they had grown even closer. Of course the tabloid press was quick to exploit Love's success in a negative way, citing tensions and jealousies between the two actresses as a disruptive element on the normally tight *Party of Five* set.

Love was bothered by those stories and would regularly point out that there was no friction between them. "People sometimes try to make it competitive between me and Neve because they assume that we both go after the same kinds of things. But I could not be more proud of a fellow actor than I am of her. She's always nice to people and she's never been anything but nice to me."

In March '98, Love once again found the time to do commercials, this time one for Neutrogena, which aired nationally. That same month her status as a rising star was validated when she was honored as Top Newcomer at the prestigious Blockbuster Awards.

"My schedule's a little bit busier now," she agreed. "I get a little less sleep and people come up to me on the street more often. But I love it. It's really nice. There's not a cloud high enough for me to be on at the moment."

Love passed through the summer and fall months on the highest of highs. She was up to her eyeballs in satisfying work and was deeply in love with a wonderful man. The year had been the perfect cap to what she considered the first phase of a bright and shining future [with Will].

Unfortunately, the inevitable pressures of balancing a personal and professional life ultimately took its toll on the fairy-tale relationship between Love and Will. The time they spent together became less and less and eventually the romantic side of their relationship began to unravel. Midway through 1998, the romance between one of Hollywood's favorite couples ended. Love remained closemouthed on the end of the relationship with Will but those close to the couple agreed that Love's rise to superstardom and the lack of time to be together were instrumental in their breakup.

LOVE STORY

Love insisted that Will and she would always be friends.

She did not withdraw following the breakup with Will, and was soon spotted on the arms of a number of young men, including MTV V.J. Carson Daly.

The popping of flashbulbs and shouts of recognition greeted Love as she emerged from the limo and walked down the red carpet on the night *I Still Know What You Did Last Summer* had its premiere. She walked slowly, deliberately attempting to make the experience last as long as possible. Fans yelled out her name. Love stopped and posed for photographs. She obliged a number of autograph requests.

A signal from the front of the theater indicated that the movie was about to start and Love hurried toward the entrance. She paused one final time at the door, turned and beamed a smile out to the crowd, and waved. For her legions of fans, it was a moment captured forever in time.

And for Love's story, it signaled a happy ending. And a new beginning.

8
Love Notes

NAME: Jennifer Love Hewitt

WHAT HER FRIENDS CALL HER: Love

HEIGHT: 5'2"

HAIR: Brown

EYES: Brown

FAVORITE MUSIC: Matchbox 20, Janis Joplin, Aretha Franklin

FAVORITE SPORT: Hockey

LOVE STORY

WHO SHE WOULD LIKE TO WORK WITH: Winona Ryder, Johnny Depp, Meg Ryan

FAVORITE ACTOR: Johnny Depp

FAVORITE FOOD: McDonald's cheeseburgers and fries, mushroom pizza, Pepsi and Coke

HOBBIES: Writing poetry, painting porcelain, collecting angels

FAVORITE TV SHOW: *Friends*

NAME OF CATS: Haylie and Don Juan

FANTASY *PARTY OF FIVE* EPISODE: Bailey and Sarah get married

FAVORITE PLACES TO SHOP: Gap, Banana Republic

FAVORITE DESIGNER: Vera Wang

FAVORITE COLOR OF CLOTHES: Purple

FAVORITE CLOTHES THAT SARAH WEARS: A brown turtleneck sweater

9
Love on the Line

Jennifer Love Hewitt's legions of devoted fans have crammed the information superhighway with dozens of Web-site rest stops. If you're interested in learning more about Jennifer Love Hewitt, the following Love shrines are the places to go.

THE JENNIFER LOVE HEWITT PAGE BY TEEMU

http://bonnie.tky.hut.fi/love/love/.html

Finland, of all places, offers quite a good mixture of quicktime videos, photos, and biographical information.

LOVE ACCESS: THE ONLINE MAGAZINE ABOUT JENNIFER LOVE HEWITT

http://home.sol.no/hestvedt/

LOVE STORY

Fun stuff like fan of the month, Love sightings, and a Love trading post combine with frequently updated information and news on Love make this one of the better one-stop shops for all things Love.

THE LOVE HEWITT SHRINE

http://www.geocities.com/Hollywood/5560

Biographical information, a solid photo gallery, and a maddening array of Love trivia. More about Love than anybody has a right to know.

THE *PARTY OF FIVE*/JENNIFER LOVE HEWITT/NEVE CAMPBELL PAGE

http://www.geocities.com/Hollywood/Hills/9912

Love and Neve share this collection of photos and biographical information.

TRIBUTE TO LOVE

http://po5gal.simplenet.com/love.html

Good photos, a complete biography, and an address where you can write Love.

THE DANISH JENNIFER LOVE HEWITT PAGE

http://w11648.telia.com/~u164800231/index.htm

Love on the Line

A good biography, some great fashion and *I Know What You Did Last Summer* photos make this Web site worth a look-see.

JENNIFER LOVE HEWITT PHOTO GALLERY

http://www.dragonhunter.com/love.html

Lots of photos from various points in Love's career.

JLH FAN'S JENNIFER LOVE HEWITT RESOURCE CENTER

http://www.geocities.com/Hollywood/Boulevard/9676

Good photos but the attention to news is the big attraction here.

MCAULY'S JENNIFER LOVE HEWITT PAGE

http://www.geocities.com/Hollywood/2808/jlh.html

The basics. Okay photos and your basic biography.

THE JENNIFER LOVE HEWITT FANSITE

http://www.geocities.com/Madison Avenue/5484/

Good bio and good photos.

LOVE STORY

THE LOVE PAGE

http://members.tripod.com/~

A modest but spirited collection of photos as well as a jumping-off point to their links.

JENNIFER LOVE HEWITT

http:members.aol.com/magsea3103/love_hewitt.html

The basic biography, one great picture, and links to other links.

THE UNOFFICIAL JENNIFER LOVE HEWITT PAGE

http://www.geocities.com/Hollywood/Studio/1685

Regular news updates highlight here. Good photos a bonus.

JENNIFER LOVE HEWITT SOURCE

http://www.geocities.com/Hollywood/Boulevard/2822/jenny.html

This is one of the more ambitious Web sites. For your click-on you get updated news, pictures, a biography, info on her movies, article transcripts, and blowups of Love magazine covers.

SKY GALLERY JENNIFER LOVE HEWITT EXHIBIT

http://www.safari.net/sky gallery/love

A good collection of photos from the recent past.

BYRDS OF PARADISE EPISODE GUIDE

http://www.tardis.ed. ac.uk/~dave/guides/Byrds OfParadise/index.html

Everything you need to know about a blip in Love's career: Cast list, story lines of each episode, and the original broadcast schedule.

The following *Party of Five* Web sites also offer information on Love as well as the ongoing evolution of Sarah Reeves.

THE OFFICIAL FOX NETWORK PARTY OF FIVE WEB SITE

http://www.foxworld.com/po5indx.htm

THE OFFICIAL SONY PARTY OF FIVE WEB SITE

http://www.spe.sony.com/Pictures/tv/party/party.html

TK BALTIMORE'S PARTY OF FIVE WEB SITE

http://www.cat.nyu.edu/tkbalt/salingers/

LOVE STORY

CLOSER TO FREE

http://rhf.bradley.edu/~violet/party.html

EVERYTHING *PARTY OF FIVE*

http://digiserve.com/kmisle/epof.html

THE SALINGERS

http://www.geocities.com/Hollywood/8061/party.html

DAVID'S *PARTY OF FIVE* PAGE

http://www.ozemail.com.au/~ryork/pof/pof.htm

THE FIRST ENGLISH *PARTY OF FIVE* PAGE

http://www.stuweeks.u-net.com/epo5.htm

MAX'S *PARTY OF FIVE* PAGE

http://www.geocities.com/Television City/4812